THE ITALIAN'S FINAL REDEMPTION

THE ITALIAN'S FINAL REDEMPTION

JACKIE ASHENDEN

MILLS & BOON

First published in Great Britain 2020
by Mills & Boon, an imprint of HarperCollins*Publishers*
1 London Bridge Street, London, SE1 9GF

www.harpercollins.co.uk

HarperCollins*Publishers*
1st Floor, Watermarque Building, Ringsend Road
Dublin 4, Ireland

Large Print edition 2021

© 2020 Jackie Ashenden

ISBN: 978-0-263-28841-4

MIX
Paper from
responsible sources
FSC˚ C007454

This book is produced from independently certified
FSC™ paper to ensure responsible forest management. For
more information visit www.harpercollins.co.uk/green.

Printed and bound in Great Britain
by CPI Group (UK) Ltd, Croydon, CR0 4YY

To JA. For true leadership.

CHAPTER ONE

LUCY ARMSTRONG HAD planned her own kidnapping meticulously.

Something simple, that wouldn't cause a fuss, and that would ultimately allow her to get away from her controlling father once and for all.

It wouldn't be easy. She was a valuable commodity to Michael Armstrong, and not for being his daughter, no, that was the very least of it. A tutor her father had hired for her had discovered she was a genius with numbers and had understood money from an early age, and had passed that discovery on to her father. He'd soon found a use for her, making sure she laundered all that ill-gotten money, and he would definitely not let her go without a fight. He guarded her assiduously and jealously, the same way he'd guarded her mother.

However, Lucy only needed an hour's physical freedom, long enough for her to implement stage two of her three-stage plan.

Stage two being to throw herself on the mercy of her father's enemy.

Stage three to request that he kidnap her and hide her for the short amount of time it would take to ensure that she disappeared without a trace so Michael would never find her again.

It wasn't the best plan she could come up with—she didn't like relying on other people— but her mother's death could not be in vain. Lucy had made a promise to her mother before she'd died, that she wouldn't let herself be kept a prisoner the way her mother had been. That she would get away from Michael, no matter what the cost. And of the few other scenarios she'd run, this one was most likely to keep her out of her father's clutches for ever.

Or so she hoped. She'd allowed for all kinds of variables, and could predict most things with surety, but she couldn't account for everything.

The main variable being him.

Vincenzo de Santi. Her father's enemy number one.

She'd done her research. The de Santis were an old and infamous Italian crime family for whom her father had once worked—at least until the matriarch had been imprisoned and her son, Vincenzo, took over. Then his crusade against the big crime families of Europe began.

One by one Vincenzo had taken them down and turned them in, including his own mother, it was reputed. The de Santi business empire—once a hotbed of white-collar crime—had been cleaned out, all sources of corruption and illegal activity removed. Now it was the very model of a business that excelled. Legally.

Vincenzo de Santi had been ruthless in his quest to drag his family back over to the right side of the law, and with other families in his sights he'd made a lot of enemies. Including her father, who hated him and had sworn to take him down.

Which made him both the perfect target and the perfect refuge.

Lucy peered up at the old, graceful ivy-covered building opposite the bus stop she was currently sitting in.

She'd managed to get hold of de Santi's schedule, and his visit to London to check on several of his family's businesses was timely, not to mention useful—for her plan to work she had to talk to him directly and not be dismissed by flunkeys. Right now he was checking on one of his family's auction houses and she'd decided this was the perfect place to throw herself on his mercy. Far less security than the big skyscraper near the river and it was in a quieter area of the city.

Still, she didn't have a lot of time. The security detail that followed her wherever she went had no doubt already figured out that she hadn't gone to powder her nose after all and were tearing up the cafe she'd insisted they stop at trying to find her.

And find her they would, she had no illusions about that.

Which meant she needed to get to stage two of her plan, and quickly.

Keeping her head down, Lucy hurried across the road to the de Santi auction house and pushed through the ornate double doors.

It was cool inside, her footsteps echoing on the marble floor as she walked towards the reception desk. A nearby waiting area was furnished with richly upholstered couches, but there was no one currently waiting. There were pictures on the walls, sculptures on the tables and various other precious items displayed in cases. Silence permeated the place. The kind of silence that only the astonishingly rich and important could buy.

Lucy ignored the art the way she ignored most things, keeping her attention on what was in front of her, since what was in front of her was always the most important thing, and approached the large and obviously antique reception desk.

A beautifully dressed young man sat behind it, looking intently at a paper-thin computer screen, and he glanced up as she approached, his expression pleasant and professional. 'Can I help you, miss?'

Lucy gripped the strap of her handbag tightly, her heart beating very fast. 'I need to speak to Mr de Santi immediately, please.'

The man's pleasant expression didn't change. 'Do you have an appointment?'

This part of her plan was always going to be difficult.

All she had was her name, and even though most people didn't know it, they surely knew of her existence. Or at least, Vincenzo de Santi would know of her existence.

'No,' Lucy said. 'But he'll want to see me. I'm Lucy Armstrong.'

That clearly meant nothing to the receptionist. His smile changed to one of polite refusal. 'I'm sorry, Miss Armstrong, but if you don't have an appointment I'm afraid you can't see Mr de Santi. He's a very busy man.'

She'd have only twenty minutes now. Twenty minutes and then they'd find her. They'd track her down and then she'd be dragged back to Cornwall. She wouldn't be allowed back to London again, and then her mother would have died for nothing.

Ice collected inside her, small tendrils of frost working their way through her veins. She'd become adept at ignoring her emotions, at not seeing anything but the task in front of her, which was generally numbers on a screen, the financial markets she lived and breathed. And for years that had worked very well.

But with freedom so close and the loss of it approaching fast, the fear she'd been trying to suppress was battering at the box she'd locked it in, trying to get out. It had taken her years to muster the courage to put this plan into motion. It *had* to work. She wasn't going to get another chance.

'It's Armstrong,' Lucy said, hoping her voice

was firm and not shaking. 'Lucy Armstrong. I'm Michael Armstrong's daughter.'

The man's expression still didn't change. Her father's name meant nothing to him.

She swallowed, the chill inside her deepening. She'd expected de Santi's gatekeepers to at least know of her father, but it was obvious that wasn't the case.

The fear was reaching higher, cold floodwaters threatening to drown her.

Her mother lying on the floor, blood pooling on the carpet where she'd fallen as she'd grabbed Lucy's hand.

'Promise me,' she'd gasped out. *'Promise me you'll survive long enough to get away from him. Escape, have a life, be free. I want you to be happy, darling. I don't want you to end up like me...'*

She'd promised and her mother had died right there in front of her.

Think.

Right. She couldn't freeze, couldn't let the fear get the better of her. Concentrate on the immediate problem and figure out a solution.

Although there didn't seem to be any security around, she wasn't fooled. De Santi's security team were legendary, which was part of why she'd chosen him to start with. If she made herself a threat in some way, she'd be instantly grabbed and hustled away somewhere secure.

Maybe that would be the way to go.

She was just sorting through that option, when a door behind the reception desk opened and an expensively dressed older man strode out. 'And I'll see you in hell, de Santi,' he flung over his shoulder before storming over to the exit.

The receptionist was halfway out of his chair, no doubt to soothe the other man's ruffled feathers, and Lucy saw her chance.

She was good at remaining unnoticed and, since the door to de Santi's office stood open, she moved quickly, heading straight to it.

No one stopped her.

She went in, her heart beating far too fast for comfort, turning and shutting the door quickly, and locking it for good measure. Then she turned around.

The atmosphere of luxury and astonishing amounts of money was here in this office too. No marble on the floor this time, but a thick, deep carpet in midnight blue. Dark wood panelled the walls, the lighting of various paintings on it discreet and subtle. Bookcases and display cases, a couch, a low coffee table and a huge oak desk.

There was a man behind the desk. And he was looking at her.

He said nothing.

Lucy's heart thundered in her ears. The minutes were ticking away and yet somehow she'd lost her voice. As if the man behind the desk had struck her dumb.

He wore a dark suit that had clearly been made for him, but it wasn't the suit that Lucy noticed first. It was his height and the broad width of his shoulders, and the hard plane of a very muscular chest. He was strength incarnate, the epitome of power. Although he lounged in the big leather chair as if waiting for a boring meeting to finish, one ankle resting on the opposite knee, he radiated that power like a king, all determination and purpose and casual arrogance.

She blinked, a feeling of safety filtering through her.

Yes, she'd been right to come here. If there

was anyone on earth who could protect her from her father, it was this man.

He still didn't say anything, watching her with eyes so dark they verged on black.

He wasn't handsome, though he possessed a powerful and undeniable charisma. It was there in his deeply set eyes, in the hard cast of his jaw, high cheekbones and straight nose. An aristocrat turned crusader. The air of ruthlessness around him made him utterly compelling.

Are you sure you were right to come here?

But Lucy shoved the thought away. She couldn't start second-guessing now.

This was Vincenzo de Santi himself and it was time to implement the next stage of her plan.

She forced herself to walk forward to the desk, stopping in front of it just as someone rattled the handle of the office door.

'Mr de Santi!' a voice called from outside.

She swallowed and said very quickly, before Security came bursting through that door, 'Mr de Santi, my name is Lucy Armstrong and I'm here because I need your protection.'

De Santi ignored the shouting and simply

watched her with no more than minor curiosity. And said nothing.

'Mr de Santi!' The door rattled again. 'I'm
calling Security right now!'

He stirred, as if only mildly bothered. 'No
need, Raoul,' he called back, his English lightly
accented, his voice deep and cold. 'Security are
already aware.' He sounded bored.

Except the black gaze that speared her was
not.

He is dangerous.

Fear moved through her again and she had to
force it down hard. That was the problem with
strong men. Strength meant safety but it could
also mean danger, as she knew all too well. Especially for her.

He was a fanatic, the rumours said. He
couldn't be swayed and he couldn't be bought.
He was incorruptible and merciless against his
enemies.

You are his enemy.

She was. But she had no other choice. She
couldn't go to the authorities, not when she
was a criminal herself, and that limited her options. Vincenzo de Santi was the only one who
could keep her safe, she had no doubt. Anyway,

though he was dangerous, he couldn't be more dangerous than her father, surely?

'Mr de Santi,' Lucy said, preparing her speech again, in case he hadn't heard her the first time, 'my name is—'

'I know who you are,' he interrupted in the same bored, calm way.

'Oh.' She was a little nonplussed. If he knew who she was already, then shouldn't he be more…interested? Wouldn't the daughter of his enemy simply walking into his office make him pleased? Certainly he should have been asking her questions. Except he wasn't. He was simply sitting there, at his leisure, in that big black leather chair. Staring at her.

It was unnerving.

Lucy shifted on her feet. She wasn't used to being stared at the way he was staring at her. As if those dark eyes were X-rays and they could see right through her clothes to her skin and deeper, right through her flesh, down to her bones.

You're freezing again. Don't get distracted, keep your attention on the goal.

That's right, she had to concentrate. The minutes were ticking away and she didn't know what would happen when her father's men burst in here. They might drag her away and she didn't want that, at least not before she'd put her proposition to him.

Steeling herself, Lucy pushed her glasses up her nose and stared right back. 'If you know who I am then you'll also know who my father is. I need your protection, Mr de Santi, and I'm willing to pay handsomely for it.'

'I see.' He didn't look at all surprised at this, nor one whit less bored. 'Please explain why I should give you anything at all.'

But Lucy didn't have the time to answer questions. She knew what she was bringing to his door in coming here: a war. No more and no less, and he needed to know immediately.

'I'll explain when you've agreed. You probably have ten minutes before my father's men track me down and come pouring through your door ready to drag me home.'

Vincenzo de Santi didn't react. He remained in his chair, his hands loosely clasped in his lap. Her father favoured big gold rings, but this man wore no jewellery. He was austere as a monk. Except monks generally did not have eyes that glittered like polished onyx; he reminded her of a great black panther about to pounce.

Time was going faster and faster, and the fear was harder and harder to contain. She gripped on to the strap of her handbag for dear life, her nails digging into her palm, the slight pain holding panic at bay.

This was obviously deliberate, this silence he was giving her. Hoping to rattle her possibly. Well, she wouldn't be rattled and she wouldn't panic. She'd got this far and she couldn't allow herself to fail.

Failure was her mother dying in a pool of blood after trying to protect her from her father's wrath, and she couldn't let that death be in vain. She wouldn't.

'Please,' she said. 'I am throwing myself on your mercy.'

The young woman—it was difficult to tell her age, given the quantity of dark hair covering most of her face, but he thought she was a woman rather than a girl—was plainly terrified, yet trying very hard not to show it. The knuckles of her right hand where it clutched the strap of a ratty brown leather handbag were white, and her skin was very pale. Her eyes behind her glasses were very large and an indeterminate colour between brown and green, and she wore a shapeless dress of the same muddy colour.

Vincenzo eyed her. Silence was a useful interrogation tactic and so he used it often. People didn't like it. It made them uncomfortable. It made them want to fill the dreadful quiet any way they could, letting slip all kinds of interesting information.

Not that Miss Lucy Armstrong was someone he was interrogating.

At least, not yet.

'Mercy,' he said, tasting the word, because it was strange to hear it used in conjunction with himself. 'I'm afraid if it's mercy you're wanting, Miss Armstrong, you've come to the wrong place.'

Her gaze, for all that it was trapped behind two pieces of thick glass, was startlingly direct. In fact, he couldn't recall a woman—or, indeed, anyone—staring at him the way she was staring at him. People were generally too afraid to look him in the eye, and with good reason.

She should be afraid too. Especially being Michael Armstrong's daughter.

He'd tried to take down that particular piece of scum for years now, but the man had evaded all Vincenzo's attempts to bring him to justice. And Vincenzo had tried *very* hard to bring him to justice. A couple of centuries ago, when crime families warred against each other, the war was carried out physically and brutally, and the authorities left well alone if they knew what was good for them. It had a certain...efficiency about it.

These days though, the battles were conducted on twenty-first-century battlefields; online, in the financial markets, in numbers and money. In shell companies and tax havens.

Vincenzo had tried many times to shut down the lucrative money-laundering business Armstrong had going on, since money and all the ways to hide it was a relatively easy way to take down someone's illegal empire. Yet every time Vincenzo thought he had Armstrong, the man managed to get away. It was puzzling.

Armstrong wasn't a subtle man and Vincenzo was almost positive he didn't have the kind of understanding required to evade Vincenzo's team of financial forensic specialists, yet somehow he did. One would almost suspect that Armstrong himself was far more sneaky than anyone thought, but Vincenzo didn't think he was. What Armstrong had was help. And Vincenzo thought he knew who that help might be.

The woman standing in front of his desk right now.

There had been many rumours throughout the European underground about Armstrong's daughter. That he guarded her closely, jealously, because she was the secret of the success of his empire. She knew numbers and money, was a genius with computers, could hide anyone's digital tracks with ease...

A dangerous woman. Yet she didn't look very dangerous. She looked very small, her body hidden away behind that awful, shapeless dress and thick, dark, frizzy hair hanging over her face. Her features were mostly hidden too, behind those thick glasses, but he thought he could see a scattering of freckles over her nose.

Not dangerous, perhaps. Just very, very unremarkable.

Interesting, though, that she should come

here. That she should blunder through his doors seeking him. His security had informed him of her presence the moment she'd set foot in his family's auction house and despite his inclination to have her instantly taken and imprisoned, since her arrival was the kind of windfall he couldn't pass up, he'd decided to let whatever she was here for play out.

Raoul needed the practice in dealing with difficulties anyway.

Lucy Armstrong took another step forward, still holding his gaze. There was a certain ferocity to her, a determination that on another day he might have admired.

But he wasn't going to admire her. She was Armstrong's partner in crime, fully complicit in his evil empire, and so he would use her instead. Get her to reveal all her father's secrets, and once Armstrong was in prison, where he belonged, she would join him.

'Mr de Santi—' she began yet again, her voice low and slightly husky.

'Don't worry, Miss Armstrong,' he interrupted. 'Your father's men won't even get through the front door. My security is excellent.' And it was, because it needed to be.

When you were conducting a crusade against the most powerful crime families in Europe, having people try to kill you was an everyday occurrence.

It didn't bother him. If people were trying to kill him it meant he was doing something right.

'You don't understand,' she said. 'He will—'

'No.' Vincenzo didn't raise his voice, didn't put any emphasis on it. Just let it cut across her, cold as an icicle. 'He will not.'

Her mouth opened then closed. It was, Vincenzo couldn't help noticing, a rather full and soft-looking mouth.

'Now,' he went on, dismissing the observation and nodding at the chair near his desk. 'Sit.'

She frowned, a deep crease between two straight dark brows, and he thought she might be working herself up to argue with him. But, clearly thinking better of it, she did as she was told, holding her worn handbag protectively in her lap.

He tilted his head, studying her. She was still very afraid. He could almost smell it on her. He was a connoisseur of fear. He knew how it worked and what it did to people, and how it could be used to manipulate them. He himself didn't use it that way, since that was an approach he loathed above all others. But he wasn't averse to people letting themselves be manipulated by their own emotions. And he was constantly amazed by the fact that they did.

Another reason, if he needed one, that it wasn't a gun that would kill you, it was fear. Or hate. Or anger. Or love. Emotions were far more dangerous than any weapon.

'Explain,' he said, finally breaking the silence that had fallen. 'Why are you here, Miss Armstrong? Apart from throwing yourself on my non-existent mercy?'

She was sitting in the chair completely rigid, almost vibrating with tension. 'But my father's men will be here any minute.'

Fear, again. And she was right to be scared. Coming to him directly would be a betrayal her father would not forgive.

He glanced at his computer screen and, sure enough, she wasn't wrong. Some of Armstrong's thugs were already at the doors of the auction house.

Vincenzo touched a button on his keyboard

and swivelled the screen around so it was in front of her. 'Top right-hand corner is a camera feed of the front of the building. As you can see, your father's men are already here. But they are being dealt with.'

It was clear he'd get nothing out of her until she was satisfied that she was safe from her father, so he might as well let her watch the proceedings. It would also serve as a good reminder to her that he was no less dangerous.

She watched the camera feed avidly, her eyes unblinking from behind her glasses. She didn't move, clutching her handbag and looking like nothing so much as a small brown owl.

Fanciful of him. And he wasn't given to fancies. Nor was he given to mercy for small, unremarkable women, who also happened to be accessories to the crimes committed by their father.

Really, he didn't know why he was letting her sit there watching a feed of his security team dealing with her father's men. Especially when what he should be doing was to call his head of Security and get Alessio to hand her over to the British police immediately. After all, if his crusade against the crime families of Europe had taught him anything it was that immediate action was the best kind of action.

Then again, she could be useful to him in all kinds of ways, especially if he wanted to eventually bring Armstrong down. Perhaps he wouldn't be calling Alessio quite yet.

'Seen enough?' he asked, watching her.

She glanced at him, frowning ferociously. 'How do you know that your security dealt with it? You didn't look once.'

'I don't need to. My team is the best there is.' He swivelled the screen back. 'Your explanation, if you please.'

She took a little breath. 'Okay. So, as I said, I'm here because I need your protection against my father. I managed to get away from him, but he'll never let me go free. He'll come for me whether I want to go back or not, and the only way to stay safe from him is to have someone to protect me. Which is where you come in.'

'Lucky me,' he said dryly. 'Presumably you know who I am, Miss Armstrong? I mean, you didn't wander into my office at random looking for a place to hide?'

The look she gave him was almost offended. 'Of course I know who you are. I planned my escape meticulously, including coming to you. You're my father's enemy number one. You're powerful and strong, and you have a great many resources. You don't owe my father anything and apparently you can't be bought.' She pushed her glasses up her nose again in what was obviously a nervous gesture. 'You're incorruptible, which makes you perfect.'

She had done her homework, hadn't she?

'I'm not as perfect as I'm sure you'd like me to be,' he said flatly. 'What's to stop me from taking you direct to the authorities right now, for example? You're an accessory to a great many crimes, Miss Armstrong, and, as you're no doubt aware, it is my stated aim to make sure people like you and your father are brought to justice swiftly.'

Her frown turned into a scowl. 'I am *not* like my father.'

'And yet you're complicit in a number of illegal activities if my sources are correct, and they usually are.'

She went even whiter than she was already, making the dusting of freckles across her nose stand out, and highlighting the shadows beneath her eyes.

Now the little owl wasn't just afraid, she was terrified.

Vincenzo had a reputation for ruthlessness, and some would have called him cruel. He supposed they could be correct about that. His world was a very black and white one, and it needed to be, since his personal mission in life didn't allow time to debate moral quandaries or sort out grey areas. He turned everyone over to the authorities and let them sort the innocent from the guilty, which could be interpreted as cruelty by some people.

It didn't bother him. He didn't care how other people interpreted his actions.

And he wasn't sure what the strange tightness was that whispered through him when he looked at the terrified young woman sitting across his desk. But it was there all the same. It was almost like…pity.

Her chin came up then, her narrow shoulders squaring slightly, as if she were facing down a firing squad.

'Yes,' she said. 'You're right, I am complicit. But prisoners don't get choices, especially when they're being threatened, and I didn't have the luxury of refusing. Believe me or don't, it's up to you. Just promise me that you will keep me safe from my father.'

She was wrong. Everyone had a choice, even if you didn't like the choice you were given.

'And why would I promise you a single thing?' he enquired, keeping the question casual.

Her gaze turned ever more determined. 'Because I can give you everything you need to take my father down.'

CHAPTER TWO

LUCY HAD KNOWN nothing but fear for most of her life and was used to it. But the fear that gripped her as she sat opposite Vincenzo de Santi was unlike any she'd ever known.

And she couldn't work out why.

Her father's men had been dealt with efficiently—she'd seen just how efficiently on that camera feed—and so there shouldn't have been any reason for her to remain scared. Yet she was, and now it had less to do with her father than it did with the man sitting opposite her.

He was still lounging there in that casual pose, to all intents and purposes bored. But his eyes glittered like black jewels and they did not move from her face, not even once. He was all coiled menace and a ruthlessness that she could almost feel like ice against her skin.

She hadn't expected to be confronted about her own crimes, not so soon, though in retrospect she should have. But she didn't like having to think about the things her father had made her do and, since she was very good at not thinking about certain things, she'd simply pushed it out of her head to be dealt with later.

Except later had now come. And Vincenzo de Santi calmly stating that she was complicit in her father's crimes wasn't something she could deny.

But she'd told de Santi the truth. She hadn't been given a choice. It was either she did what her father asked, or there were consequences. Survive, that was what her mother had told her and so that was what she'd done, any way she could.

Maybe one day there would be time to address her crimes, but she would see her father taken down first if it was the last thing she did.

Yet it wasn't her guilt or otherwise which scared her. It was something else. Something about Vincenzo de Santi himself that she couldn't put her finger on.

She wasn't used to men. Her father kept her secluded in Cornwall, her every move watched by the guards he employed twenty-four-seven. She had a few online friends, but she made sure any identities she used online were heavily cloaked. She didn't really see anyone but the guards in real life, and she kept away from them, because they made her uncomfortable. It would have been a lonely existence if she'd let herself think about it, but she didn't ever let herself think about it. Never let herself see the bars of the cage she was locked in. Never contemplated the tightrope she walked between being useful enough for her father so he'd keep her alive, and refusing to do certain things that would anger him and make him deal out the same punishment he'd given her mother.

Her attention must always be on what was directly in front of her, never looking right or left, or anywhere else. Otherwise she would lose her balance and fall to her death.

She stared hard at Vincenzo de Santi, not letting her focus waver, not paying any attention to the new fear that lived inside her, just under her skin. An electric, prickling kind of fear that made her heart beat fast.

'Of course, you will give me everything you have on your father,' de Santi said easily, as if that had always been a foregone conclusion. 'Immediately, if you please.'

Lucy eyed him warily. 'And you will then hand me over to the police?'

He lifted one powerful shoulder and she found herself watching the way the fabric of his suit jacket pulled in response to the movement. She didn't know why. She already knew he was strong; she didn't need to watch him in order to confirm that.

'Naturally.' He put one hand on the arm of his chair, one long finger tapping out a soundless, slow, meditative rhythm. 'I should imagine the police would be very happy to get their hands on you.'

They probably would. But she didn't want to go. She hadn't survived for years waiting for her chance to escape, only to be put back in yet another cage. That wasn't what her mother had wanted for her.

But you have committed crimes. You deserve prison.

It was true. And to a certain extent she'd protected herself from the knowledge of what she'd done by not enquiring too deeply about where all her father's money had come from. Because she knew, if she did, she'd discover things that would make her life even more untenable than it was already. So she hadn't enquired. She'd only done what she was told. She'd made some money disappear into offshore accounts, pouring the rest into other investments, making her father's bank balances grow.

It had been survival, pure and simple.

But did survival really deserve a jail cell?

Because Vincenzo de Santi would hand her over to the police, that was obvious. She could see it in his mesmerising, compelling face. He was her judge, jury and executioner, and she couldn't look away.

Her hands tightened on her handbag and the laptop hidden in it. The laptop that contained all the information he required. But not the passwords he would need. Those were all in her head.

'When you say you will hand me over to the police, when will that happen?' It was very difficult, but she held his gaze. Because she had to know. His handing her over to the authorities had always been a possibility, but she'd held out a tiny sliver of hope that perhaps he wouldn't. That he'd help her disappear into obscurity somewhere in the US, far away from her father. Where she could make sure her mother's death hadn't been in vain.

He tilted his head and she had the impression that he could see every single part of her. From her guilty conscience to the fear she lived with every day. Every aspect of her small, narrow, confined existence.

'You give me the information I want,' he said in that easy, casual voice, 'and then I will notify the authorities. This afternoon probably. The quicker you do it, the quicker I can take your father off the streets for good.'

Perhaps he'd meant that to be encouraging, or maybe an incentive for her. But it wasn't.

And her expression must have given her away, which was a shock in itself, since no one ever noticed her emotions, because he said, 'This does not please you?' His mouth curved slightly and she found herself watching that too, as if she was compelled. 'But Miss Armstrong, if you'd done your research you would know that I do not care for criminals. And, as I've already told you, if it's mercy you're looking for, you'll find I have none.'

She'd underestimated him. She'd thought that perhaps she would be unimportant to him. That her father would be his ultimate goal and he'd let her slip away to pursue her own redemption far away from the constant fear.

But she'd been so fixated on her immediate plan she'd miscalculated.

That's always been your greatest failing.

Yes, that was true.

She shifted her hold on her laptop, her fingers nervously gathering up the fabric of her dress and pleating it.

Okay, she told herself, *so don't think about what he was going to do, don't think about police cells and having to survive for years in a prison with fear your only companion yet again. Don't think about your mother dying in a pool of blood, begging you not to end up like she did.*

Only think about how to change his mind.

She steeled herself, met his black gaze head-on. 'It'll take some time to give you this information, since I don't have all the data yet. Probably, say, a week.' Was a week long enough to change his mind? She didn't think she could push for more. And the reality was that she'd have to work with whatever he gave her.

If he even gave her anything at all.

One black brow rose. 'A week?' he echoed, as if it was the most preposterous thing he'd ever heard. 'Forgive me, Miss Armstrong, but I've heard all the rumours about you. I know what you're capable of. You could get me that information in ten seconds if you wanted to.'

'But I don't want to,' she said flatly, before she could stop herself. 'A week, Mr de Santi. A week and I'll give you all you need to not only take my father down, but his entire empire along with him.'

De Santi's eyes narrowed, an obsidian blade getting sharper. So sharp it might cut. 'Why would I wait a week? In ten minutes I can make you tell me anything I want to know.'

The icy flood of fear inside her rose higher. His ruthlessness was legendary, as was his single-minded determination. He'd betrayed his own parents to the authorities, it was rumoured, which meant he would have no qualms about torturing her into giving him whatever he wanted.

Lucy gripped on to her courage, held it tight, and didn't look away. 'You can torture me all you like, Mr de Santi, but I'm not going to give you a thing.'

If being accused of potential torture bothered him, he didn't show it. 'And what makes you think you can hold out against torture, Miss Armstrong?'

Well, that was the problem. She didn't think she could. Then again, she'd doubted she'd ever be able to escape her father and yet she had, so anything was possible.

'I have a very high pain threshold,' she said, because that was true. Certainly her father wouldn't let her have painkillers, so she'd had to deal with severe period pain and migraines by herself. 'You can put glass under my nails or break my fingers, but I won't tell you a single thing.'

De Santi blinked once. 'Glass,' he murmured. 'Break your fingers... Hmm. Both good options that yield results, certainly. But I could just take that laptop you're clutching on to and save myself the drama.'

'You could,' she allowed. 'But it wouldn't do you any good. All the information on this laptop is encrypted, and the passwords are all in my head.'

The edge of his stare was pressing against her skin, cutting her.

She gritted her teeth, refusing to give in and look away. She might not know much about men, but she did know that strong men liked to test that strength on others. She'd seen her father do it with his associates and his enemies, and he enjoyed it. When he was in the mood, he even appreciated strength in others, too.

Perhaps de Santi was the same. In which case maybe letting him test his strength against her determination might buy her the time she wanted. Maybe it would even go towards him changing his mind about handing her over to the authorities.

Whatever, it was clear that remaining unnoticed and slipping beneath the radar the way she normally did wouldn't work with him. In which case, if he was going to notice her, then she couldn't allow him to see her fear, her weakness. And, since she wasn't particularly strong, she'd just have to be determined instead, and if there was one thing she was it was determined.

'Looking at me ferociously won't make me any more likely to tell you,' she said, clutching tighter to her laptop. 'I can hold out against you.'

He tilted his head, his eyes gleaming from

beneath surprisingly long, dark lashes. 'I'm sure you can. But I've broken hardened criminals, and I'm sure one small, soft one would be no bother at all.'

Was he mocking her? She couldn't tell. The expression on his brutal, aristocratic face was utterly unreadable, his gaze absolutely opaque.

He frightened her. And yet she realised that, even though she was frightened, the prickling feeling she got between her shoulder blades whenever she thought about her father had gone.

De Santi had dealt with him for now. For now, at least, she was safe.

That thought steadied her.

'You can try,' she said, glaring at him. 'I'm not afraid of you.'

'Yes, you are.' His voice was very deep and very cold, his gaze as merciless as the man himself. 'You're terrified of me.'

It was obvious she didn't like him pointing that out to her. Anger glittered in her eyes, her delicate jaw getting a stubborn cast. She opened her mouth, no doubt to deny it, but he forestalled her.

'Don't lie to me, Miss Armstrong. I can smell a lie a mile off. And I have a feeling you're not very good at it anyway.'

She bit her full bottom lip, small white teeth worrying at it. He found his gaze had fixated on that soft mouth for absolutely no reason that he could see. He liked a woman's mouth, but unless it was doing something interesting to him he wouldn't tend to notice it in the general scheme of things. Certainly not when the owner of said mouth was a criminal he was hoping to bring to justice.

He took his pleasures with women only when it suited him and did not allow himself to be subject to the whims of his body. It was true that he'd been too busy for female company the past month, mopping up the last of the St Etienne family and their drug empire, but that didn't concern him. His body might protest but he rather enjoyed such exercises in self-control. It kept him sharp.

Regardless, even if he'd been desperate he wouldn't have let his interest fall on the woman opposite. He preferred his lovers less… unkempt. And definitely not criminals.

Especially criminals who had the gall to accuse him of using torture. Which he didn't. He would never stoop to using the same tactics his own family had once employed, even if only in centuries past. He didn't need to now, anyway. When it came to information gathering, the team he'd assembled to assist him was the best in the world, and most of the time he didn't even need his quarry to be physically present. He collected the information, handed it to the police, and let them do the rest.

Miss Lucy Armstrong continued to glare at him, while at the same time her knuckles were white as she simultaneously clutched her laptop with one hand, the other gathering and releasing the fabric of her shapeless dress. 'Well?' she demanded in her sweetly husky voice, ignoring what he'd said about her fear. 'Will you give me a week or not?'

'Why should I? I can take your laptop and turn it over to my forensic specialists right now. They can crack any encryption within—'

'No, they can't,' she interrupted flatly. 'Not the encryption I put on the information on the laptop. No one can crack it except me.'

An unaccustomed irritation rippled through him. Being interrupted was not what he was used to and especially not being interrupted by people he was going to turn in.

Most especially when those people were small women who were afraid of him and yet couldn't quite stop themselves from challenging him.

It…intrigued him that she couldn't and spoke of a certain courage. Unless she was stupider than he'd initially suspected. But no, he didn't think she was stupid. A woman who'd escaped a violent crime lord like Michael Armstrong would never be stupid.

'Then you won't mind handing it over and letting my specialists take a look,' he said mildly, deciding to let the interruption go.

'Any attempts to access the data without the passwords will result in all the data being deleted automatically.' She glared owlishly at him from behind her glasses. 'So I guess if you want to risk losing it all, then that's up to you.'

No, definitely not stupid at all.

Vincenzo's irritation deepened, along with the curiosity he'd been trying not to pay any attention to. It stretched out inside him, lazy and subtle, making him think of questions. Such as, how had she managed to escape her father?

And why had she come to him now? What made her think he would protect her? If she'd done her research, she must have known he'd simply hand her over to the authorities, surely?

You could give her a week. What would it matter in the long run? You'll turn her in eventually. And in the meantime you can get everything you need to know from her about Armstrong.

It was true, he could. And there were other things he could get from her too. If she was indeed the reason Armstrong had evaded all his traps, perhaps he could use her to entrap others. Because, after all, he had a long list. And hadn't he made the decision to employ hackers in his IT section to make sure their own online security was watertight? Use a criminal to hunt down other criminals… Why not?

He was a patient man. A week was nothing.

Vincenzo studied her carefully, taking his time. He kept his finger tapping on the arm of his chair and saw her attention zero in on it. A useful distraction technique.

She was still hunched in her chair, narrow shoulders collapsing in on themselves like the wings of a bird trying to hide itself beneath its own feathers.

It didn't surprise him. Armstrong was a man much given to casual cruelty and there had been many rumours about his first wife and her death years ago. Rumours that only made Vincenzo even more determined to bring the man down.

He didn't have any particular sentimentality towards women—he knew that they could be just as ruthless and cruel as men, and he'd had personal experience of this—but he despised physical cruelty. It was the weapon of the weak, in his opinion, and he had no doubt that Michael Armstrong was one of those weak men who needed to use it in order to enforce his power over people.

Had Armstrong used it on his daughter? Was that why she was hunched in her chair trying to make herself small? Was that why she was so afraid of himself?

Why are you thinking about her like this? She's his daughter and a criminal, and now she is a tool you can use.

All very good points.

He moved, sliding his ankle off his knee

and leaning forward, elbows on the desk. He watched her reaction as he did so, observing how her eyes went wide and how she held herself very still in her chair, her knuckles whitening even further on her handbag.

Yes, this little brown bird was very afraid. And of him.

Yet, for all that, she watched him very intently, as if he was a large cat stalking her. And, yes, there was fear, but it was clear to him that she also had a stubborn, determined spirit that wouldn't let her give in. An interesting combination.

Why? Since when are you intrigued by the people you bring to justice?

Vincenzo ignored that thought, since he didn't have an answer to it. Instead, he held her fixed hazel gaze with his and said, 'You are enterprising, Miss Armstrong. I'm impressed. Your encryption might hold out against my experts or it might not. But perhaps I'm not in the mood to wait for them to break it. Perhaps I'm in the mood to make a bargain with you instead.'

Her gaze was ferocious. 'What kind of bargain?'

'Your skills are obviously valuable and I could use them, and not only to take your father down. There are plenty of other men and women just like him around. Those who need to be behind bars, and I think you could prove very useful in helping me bring them to justice.'

Those small white teeth worried at her bottom lip. It was very red now and very full, and it had the sweetest curve. A vulnerable, soft mouth. Would it taste as sweet if he took a bite out of it himself?

Why are you thinking about her mouth, fool?

The thought was sharp and bright and shocking. He had no idea why he was thinking about her mouth. None. He shouldn't have even noticed it.

'Why would I want to do that?' she asked bluntly, not noticing his sudden stillness. 'I'll help you with my father and that's all.'

Irritation rippled through him once again, his temper not helped by his own wandering thoughts. 'I'm afraid you do not have a choice.' He kept his voice flat and cold. 'If you want a week before I hand you to the authorities it will be in my custody and you will do anything I ask. That is the price. If you don't want to pay it then I will get my security team to hand you over to the police immediately.'

She bit at her lip, the expression on her face—what he could see of it behind all that hair and those big glasses—turning angry. 'But you won't be able to take down my father if I don't help you.'

'Of course I can take down your father without you.' He made a negligible gesture. 'It would only take longer. Your help would expedite the process, but it's not necessary.'

'Then why bargain with me at all?'

Another good point. She was astute, he'd give her that. Because he really didn't need to bargain with her. He could make her do whatever he wanted, since he was the one with all the power here. But doing so would make him no better than those he brought to justice, and he would never use those kinds of tactics.

'Because, although you are not necessary, you could prove to be useful,' he said, just as blunt as she was. 'And a tool is only useful if it is not broken. I have no wish to break you, Miss Armstrong, believe me.'

'But you want to use me.' There was no anger

in her tone, only a kind of...resignation. As if the situation she now found herself in wasn't unfamiliar.

And it wouldn't be. She was as much a tool for him as she was for her father and he was very aware of that fact. Not that it bothered him. Not given what was at stake.

The old crime families of Europe were like a disease, rotting the body from the inside. Corrupting everything. That corruption was inside himself too and he knew it. Knew his own family's history and the stain they'd left behind them over the centuries.

He wasn't exempt from that corruption, but at least he wasn't here to hasten its spread. No, he was a surgeon and he would cut it out completely.

'No, *civetta*,' he said, because a surgeon needed a sharp scalpel, 'I do not want to use you. I *will* use you. If you want your week of freedom, then you must pay for it and that is my price.'

She continued to stare at him, frowning, as if he was a problem she wanted to solve. 'When you say "freedom", what exactly do you mean?'

she asked. 'Because you won't be letting me go, I assume.'

'No, I'm afraid not.'

She only nodded, as if that was the answer she'd expected. 'Well, I suppose if I were truly free that would leave me unprotected, which would undermine the whole point of me coming to you in the first place.' The line between her brows seemed etched there, marring her pale skin, and he found himself idly wondering if that skin was as soft as it looked. Whether it would be as soft as her mouth. 'I wouldn't like to be in a cell,' she went on. 'My father kept me in his house in Cornwall with a lot of guards. I could walk in the garden but that was it. It was by the ocean, but the house had no view so I couldn't see it. I could hear it though.' A thread of some emotion he couldn't place crept into her voice. 'I'd like to be able to see the waves.' Her gaze had turned distant, looking through him as if he wasn't there. 'In fact, I don't think I've ever seen the ocean. How ridiculous is that? When we live on an island?'

Slowly, Vincenzo leaned back in his chair, studying her. A strange criminal indeed to escape her father, throwing herself on his non-existent mercy then demanding his protection despite her obvious terror, only to talk with wistfulness about an ocean she'd never seen.

Perhaps it was an act. One could never tell. People of her ilk were liars and used all kinds of emotional tricks to get what they wanted. Already he was thinking odd thoughts about her mouth and about her skin… Thoughts he'd never normally have about a woman like this one. He'd encountered women who'd used seduction as a way to get close to him, either to murder him or manipulate him for other reasons. Women who weren't aware that their techniques wouldn't work on him. He was impossible to manipulate, especially when it came to emotions, because he didn't have any.

A lesson he'd learned the hard way. From his mother. A lesson this woman, this little brown owl, would soon learn too. Also the hard way.

So what are you going to do with her, then?

A good question. She was either exactly what she seemed and relatively harmless apart from the information she carried in her head, or she was far more dangerous than she appeared. Either way he would need to watch her closely.

'Prisoners do not get to determine what cell

they prefer,' he said after a moment. 'That is what being a prisoner means.'

The line between her brows was deep, a carved furrow of worry or of concentration. Or maybe both. 'I know what being a prisoner means, believe me. I guess it's too much to ask for a week of a normal life.'

Vincenzo frowned. 'A normal life? Is that what you were expecting when you came to me? That I would simply let you go?'

Her gaze behind her glasses wavered, colour staining her cheeks, softening the drawn look on her face. 'Yes. I was hoping that you would help me…disappear, if I gave you the information you want.'

'Disappear?

'You give me a new identity, help me get to the States or somewhere else, away from Dad. And then I could vanish where no one would ever find me.'

For a second all Vincenzo could do was stare at her, conscious of a certain shock echoing through him. Did she really think he would help her? That she, a known criminal, would put herself in terrible danger simply on the expectation that he would do exactly what she asked? She was either very stupid or very arrogant, or maybe a combination of both.

Then again, as he'd already thought, she wasn't stupid. And the woman huddled in her chair in an ugly dress with her hair in her eyes definitely didn't seem arrogant either.

Perhaps she's telling the truth. Perhaps she genuinely thought you would save her.

A foolish belief. He wasn't in the business of saving people. He was in the business of delivering them to justice. And if she thought she would be different, then she was wrong. Mercy was a luxury he couldn't afford.

'Then I'm afraid you're destined for disappointment,' he said, keeping his voice hard. 'You should have been more thorough with your research, Miss Armstrong. I keep telling you that I am not a merciful man. You should have listened.' He pushed himself out of his chair and strolled around the desk towards the door.

Her eyes had gone very wide and she didn't move, obviously frozen in place by fear. A gentler man might have felt sorry for her, but he had no gentleness left in him.

He crushed the ghost of that strange emotion

he'd suspected was pity. Crushed it flat completely. Then he unlocked his office door and opened it. 'Get Security, Raoul,' he ordered casually, not raising his voice. 'This prisoner needs a cell.'

CHAPTER THREE

LUCY SHIVERED. A cell.

There had been a few times when she hadn't wanted to do what her father had told her, when she'd pushed against the bars imprisoning her, and his response had always been the same. Since she was too valuable for him to kill or maim, he would drag her down to the basement in that house in Cornwall—or get one of his guards to do it—and lock her in one of the tiny rooms there. The room had no windows and when the door closed the darkness was absolute. A crushing weight that stole her breath. She never knew how long he would leave her there, but it always felt like aeons.

She hated the darkness. Hated that room. And without fail, whenever he dragged her out of it, she would always do what he asked. Until eventually she learned to always do what he asked every time.

She'd thought that when she'd escaped her father she'd leave that room behind her for ever. It seemed she was wrong.

Vincenzo de Santi had always been the variable she couldn't predict and yet she should have been able to. She'd ascribed to him a morality that it was clear he didn't have, and in retrospect she didn't even know why she'd thought he would help her in the first place.

He was everything the rumours had said about him. Cold, incorruptible, ruthless. Without a shred of mercy. He stood there staring at her, so tall, so powerful, a certain cold, brutal beauty to him that her stupid brain couldn't help appreciating even as everything inside her felt as if it was collapsing in terror.

You're not brave, not like your mother.

No, that was true. She wasn't. She was made of fear instead and that fear in turn had made her stupid. She'd thought that the knowledge in her head would be worth more to him than her physical presence. More than the weight of her own crimes.

She was wrong.

'Please.' The word was a scraped thread of sound, which was all she could muster up. 'Not a cell.'

Begging now?

Her mother hadn't begged. Her mother had been fearless, stepping between her and her enraged father, taking the blow that had been meant for her.

She could only dream of being that brave, that strong.

The sound of footsteps came and two security guards dressed in black appeared in the doorway. She knew how skilled they were. She'd watched them in the camera feed de Santi had shown her. There was no escape for her. There never had been.

Always, in every way, she was trapped.

Fear had locked all her muscles, her breathing getting faster. They would drag her away, wouldn't they? Drag her into a hole, into the darkness, and she would be trapped there. It was like dying, that darkness. A weight that would crush all the life and the breath out of her...

The guards came towards her and her vision wavered, turning black around the edges. The darkness was coming for her. It would swallow her whole.

She opened her mouth to scream but there

was no air in her lungs, no air anywhere, and she was falling, falling into that blackness, and there was no end to it...

'Breathe, *civetta*,' a deep, cold voice ordered in her ear. 'Breathe.'

It was to be obeyed, that voice. It brooked no argument. So she tried, sucking in air, pushing back against the crushing weight on her chest and the darkness pressing in.

A wave of dizziness caught her, making her tremble. She was so cold. She couldn't feel her fingers or her toes.

'Breathe,' the voice ordered again, and so she did.

More dizziness and she was trembling even harder. But something was around her, something strong. Something hot. Holding her. The heat made her feel less cold and she was held very tightly, which seemed to ease the shaking.

A warm scent surrounded her, cedar and sandalwood, oddly comforting, and she could have sworn she could hear the beating of someone's heart. It was strong and steady and slow, and she found herself trying to breathe to match that rhythm. In fact, if she concentrated, it steadied the frantic race of her own heartbeat too.

Gradually the tight pull of her muscles relaxed and the cold feeling in her hands and feet began to ease, the weight on her chest lifting. Everything was still dark, but as her consciousness returned she gradually realised that it was because her eyes were closed.

And then she realised something else: that the thing holding her was a person and the strong bands around her were arms. That the warmth was someone's body. She was lying against someone and it was their heart she could hear beating.

Shock rippled through her.

'Breathe,' the voice reminded, a deep rumble in her ear.

So she breathed and kept on breathing as she became conscious of more, that she was being held by someone very strong and very hot, and that the warmth of their body was helping her to relax, making the panic—and it had definitely been panic—recede.

Strange how the fact of being held made her feel safe, because she definitely did feel safe. And that was an unfamiliar feeling in itself, since it had been a long time since she'd felt safe anywhere. So she held on to it, kept it tight in her grasp, not wanting to move, not even wanting to breathe in case the feeling disappeared.

But she had to breathe and she kept on breathing, and she became aware of where she was. Of what had happened. Of whose arms surrounded her and who it must be holding her so tightly.

Vincenzo de Santi. Who was going to put her in a cell.

Lucy opened her eyes.

She was sitting on a sofa in the same expensive, luxurious office she remembered, in the lap of the same man who'd stared at her so intensely from across that big desk. A man with black eyes and the face of a warrior angel.

His powerful arms were around her and she was leaning against his chest as if it were her favourite pillow. Her glasses were gone and everything was blurry, but she remembered those eyes and that face. They would haunt her dreams.

She must have had a panic attack. How humiliating.

And then she realised that two other men were standing in front of the sofa, dressed in black uniforms. Tall, powerful men... The guards, come to take her away.

Instantly cold fear poured through her veins, her hands clutching on to de Santi's shirt, and she was pressing herself against him, as if he could keep her safe.

You idiot. He's the one who wants to imprison you.

Her fingers were going cold again and she could hear the frantic rush of someone's frightened breathing. Hers.

'Out,' de Santi ordered flatly, then said something else, deep and low in fluid Italian.

The guards instantly turned and left the office, closing the door behind them.

'Keep breathing,' he murmured. 'Relax your muscles.'

Helpless to do anything else, Lucy did what he said, leaning against his very hard chest and cushioned by the expensive wool of his suit. His body was so warm and the beat of his heart was in her ear, a steady, relentless sound. She concentrated on that, since it had worked so well before, and her breathing slowed, her muscles losing their rigidity.

It was strange to be held like this. She couldn't

remember the last time anyone had held her. Not since her mother had died, certainly. She'd been around seven then, so...a long time. And definitely not by a man. Were all men this hot? This hard?

You're an idiot. He wants to put you in a cell.

The thought made her stiffen again, his arms tightening in response.

'No,' he said casually and without emphasis. 'Be still.'

And, since those arms gave her no other choice, she did so. Yet, though the panic lost its bite, the fear wouldn't go away. Not now she was fully aware of who held her and where she was. And what he was going to do.

'What happened?' she asked, her voice rusty-sounding. 'Did I faint?'

'Very briefly.'

The low rumble of his voice was oddly comforting, though she had no idea why. 'Why are you holding me?'

'Because you were shaking and you'd gone very cold.' He shifted slightly, the movement of his powerful body beneath her sending a bolt of some strange sensation through her. 'I removed your glasses for safety's sake.'

She blinked, remembering something. 'And my computer?'

'It's on the sofa beside me, along with your handbag.'

A brief silence fell.

Lucy closed her eyes again, suddenly exhausted. She'd been operating on nothing but adrenaline since she'd woken up this morning with her plan in place, and now, the panic attack having burned through all the rest of her reserves, she had nothing left.

She was literally in the arms of her enemy, the prospect of a cell in front of her, and all she wanted to do was sleep.

Pathetic. Do you really want your mother to die for nothing? Pull yourself together.

Lucy gritted her teeth and forced herself to ignore her own weariness.

'Do you have panic attacks often, Miss Armstrong?' he asked after a moment.

'Not usually.' She hadn't had one for weeks, not since she'd stopped resisting her father. But did the nightmares count? Maybe they didn't.

'What is it about a cell that frightens you?'

She hadn't wanted him to know the depth of her fear, but that ship had long since sailed.

And perhaps, if he knew, it might make him more sympathetic towards her. Useful, given the fact that she was still hoping to change his mind and have him not hand her over to the police.

'There's a room in the basement of our house in Cornwall. My father locks me in there sometimes when I won't do what I'm told. It's dark. There are no windows.' A shiver coursed through her, making de Santi's arms tighten once more.

'I see,' he said, his tone very neutral. 'And do you not do what you're told often?'

As a child, she'd been fearless and curious, always getting into things she wasn't supposed to, which had made her father angry. Her mother had shielded her from the worst of his rages—until she hadn't been able to shield her any more and Lucy found out just how much her mother had protected her.

'I used to,' she said, because there was no need to get into that. 'Not so much any more.'

'Except for escaping from him.'

'Yes, except for that.' She had relaxed against him fully now, the warmth of his body stealing through her. How could such a cold man be so warm? It didn't make any sense. 'Why are you so hot?' she asked, opening her eyes again. 'Are you sick?'

His face was blurry and she couldn't read it, but she could feel his muscles tighten beneath her as if in surprise. 'No, I'm not sick.' There was a thread of something in his tone, marring the casual sound of it, but she couldn't tell what it was. 'Are you dizzy? Still a little faint?'

'No. I'm okay now, I think.'

Instantly he moved, gathering her gently without a word and shifting her off his lap and onto the sofa. The whole of her left side where she'd been resting against him felt hot, the withdrawal of his arms like a loss, which was very strange and she didn't understand it, not one bit. A wave of sudden vulnerability flooded through her, and she fussed with her dress, hoping he hadn't noticed.

It seemed he hadn't though, because he moved over to the desk, picking something up off it and holding it out to her. Her glasses.

'Thank you,' she murmured awkwardly, taking them and putting them back on.

De Santi was leaning against his desk, his

arms folded, his dark gaze fixed on her with unnerving intensity.

Lucy wanted to stand up, not have him loom so threateningly over her, but she wasn't sure if her legs would even support her, so she stayed where she was and lifted her chin instead. 'I suppose you're now going to put me in a cell?'

'I haven't decided,' he said.

An echo of fear shivered through her once again, but she borrowed some of her mother's courage and steeled herself against it, meeting his gaze head-on. 'If it's to be a cell, then you'll have to either drug me or knock me unconscious, because I won't go in there willingly.'

'Clearly.' He continued to stare at her for a couple of moments longer, then he muttered to himself in Italian again, and abruptly reached into the pocket of his suit trousers and brought out a slim, complicated-looking phone. Pushing a button, he raised it to his ear, then began to speak in rapid Italian, his gaze still resting on her.

The feeling of unease widened. What was he going to do with her now? Would he really drug her or knock her unconscious and put her in a cell?

Then again, he'd obviously had every intention of doing just that before and he hadn't. She'd had her panic attack and, instead of simply picking her up and dumping her in whatever holding facility he'd intended to put her in, he'd held her in his lap instead. Calming her down, soothing her.

Perhaps he isn't as merciless as he told you he was?

Certainly a merciless man wouldn't have held her like that and eased her fear. A merciless man—and she knew all about merciless men—would have dumped her in that cell and left her there, panic attack or not.

Something hard inside her, a knot that had pulled so tight it felt as if she'd never get it undone, relaxed slightly. Perhaps there was hope, then. Perhaps she might change his mind after all. Perhaps she might be able to make good on the promise she'd made to her mother after all.

She swallowed, and smoothed her dress again, keeping her gaze on the green fabric while listening to the fluid lilt of his voice.

Eventually, he stopped speaking and she looked up at him. He slipped his phone back into his pocket, his dark gaze impenetrable. 'You can relax. There will be no cell for you.'

Relief swept through her and it was a good thing she was sitting down, otherwise she would have fallen. 'Oh?' she managed thickly. 'Then where will you keep me?'

'I have a house here in London. You will be going there.' His gaze was as hard and sharp as obsidian. 'It's not a cell, Miss Armstrong, but believe me, it is still a prison.'

She didn't doubt that, not for a second. Yet somehow the knot inside her had become a little less tight. It wasn't freedom, no, but at least it wasn't some dark hole where she would be left for hours on end.

'I didn't think you had any mercy left,' she said, which in retrospect probably wasn't the wisest of things to say to him.

He only looked at her, his expression as neutral as his tone. 'As I said, I don't like my tools broken. And you're no use to me if you're catatonic with fear.'

Lucy swallowed again. Perhaps she was wrong after all. Perhaps the way he'd held her and soothed her had purely been from self-interest.

Why do you care what his reasons are? You're safe. That's the only thing that matters.

It was true. And she didn't care about his reasons. She only wanted to know so she had hope that she might be able to change his mind about handing her over to the police. That hope was still there, especially if he thought of her as useful.

In which case, she would make herself as useful as she possibly could for as long as she possibly could.

'Thank you,' she said.

'Don't thank me yet.' His gaze was very intent. 'You're not going alone.'

Vincenzo took a dim view of people's emotional...difficulties. He'd encountered them many times in his little crusade for justice and they always left him cold. Some people pleaded with him, weeping and going to pieces, while others got angry, throwing punches and shouting curses. Some even did what Miss Lucy Armstrong did, collapsing in fear as their lives unravelled before their eyes.

He was always impervious. He didn't let any of those emotional storms touch him, refusing to be manipulated by tears or curses, or white-faced panic. Much of the time it was all for show anyway, people thinking they could get him to change his mind with a few moving emotional scenes. They were always wrong.

His mother had been the queen of emotional manipulation and he could see through such fakery very easily.

So he wasn't sure what had made him gather Michael Armstrong's daughter up in his arms as her eyes had rolled back into her head and she'd nearly fallen off her chair. It was just the kind of thing that some people tried to get his sympathy or his pity, and so he should have let her fall onto the ground. Or let his security drag her off to the small office bathroom he'd planned on locking her in.

Yet he hadn't. No, he'd darted forward as her glasses had fallen off her nose and she'd started to list to the side, pulling her into his arms and going to sit on the sofa with her in his lap. Holding her tight as she'd shivered and trembled. She'd been so pale, and without her glasses guarding her face he was able to see clearly the scattering of freckles across her small, straight nose. A delicate, vulnerable face, with a decidedly stubborn, pointed chin and that luscious, full mouth. Not beautiful and yet not without charm. Her lashes were long and thick and dark, the same as the untidy mass of hair flowing over his arm. And he'd been surprised by the feel of decidedly feminine curves against him. He could have sworn she'd be very slight and skinny, but she definitely wasn't. No, she was warm and soft. And then when she'd come to and had seen his guards, and had clutched at his shirt, trying to press herself closer against him, as if he could protect her…

His chest had gone oddly tight and he'd sent his security away before he'd even had a chance to think straight.

Why had he done that? Why had he held her so tightly? What on earth was the feeling that had coiled inside him, because he could have sworn he was immune to both pity and sympathy? He should have ignored her and had her dragged away, treating her panic like the award-winning performance it no doubt was…

Yet he didn't think it was a performance. Her panic had been real.

He watched her as the unmarked, nondescript car he'd used to transport them both to his house in one of the quieter parts of Kensington drew up to the kerb. Since assassination attempts were a daily part of his life and since Armstrong would now no doubt be aware of where his daughter was, Vincenzo had sent a decoy limo heading in the direction of the city, while he'd bundled Lucy and himself into another car out the back of the auction house.

There had been no incidents in the short trip and nothing out of the ordinary now as his bodyguards checked the quiet square where his house was situated. He had a few in London and he changed where he stayed with each visit.

So far no one had worked out that this place was his and so it was relatively safe. He still hadn't decided what he was going to do with her though. He had to fly back to Naples in the next couple of days to deal with a few issues with one of the de Santi business subsidiaries, and hadn't expected to be dealing with Michael Armstrong's notorious daughter. Hadn't expected to be giving her a week's reprieve from justice, either.

It interfered with his plans and he didn't like it.

The bodyguards pulled open the door and Lucy got out. He followed, striding past her and up the stairs to the front door. It opened immediately, one of his housekeepers having been alerted to his presence on the drive over.

Lucy was hustled inside and directed to the lavishly appointed sitting room at the front of the house, with the opaque windows that made looking inside very difficult.

His housekeeper had put some refreshments on a small tray—tea and some expensive chocolate chip biscuits—on a table next to one of the armchairs and Vincenzo guided Lucy over to the chair and made her sit down.

She glared crossly at him from underneath her curtain of hair, her hazel eyes looking very green behind the lenses of her glasses.

A strange woman. Almost catatonic with fear one moment then angry the next. Was this another performance for his benefit? Or had her fear been the performance? But no, it couldn't have been. He'd already decided it wasn't, hadn't he?

'Drink the tea,' he ordered. 'And have a biscuit. You could probably do with the sugar.'

'I don't want a biscuit. Or the tea.' She continued to glare at him for no reason that he could see. 'What are you going to do with me?'

He turned away, pacing over to the fireplace and stopping, laying a hand on the marble mantelpiece.

It was a good question. What *was* he going to do with her? He could leave her alone in this house for the next week, which would be the most logical thing, and have his security team get the answers he required from her. And yet…he was strangely reluctant to do so.

He'd told her that he hadn't wanted a broken tool and he hadn't lied. It had been the most likely explanation for his catching her before she'd fallen off the chair and holding her. It certainly wasn't because he felt sorry for her. No, if she was frozen with fear then he wouldn't be able to get any information out of her at all, so he'd had to do something. She was to be the scalpel with which he cut out the corruption that was Michael Armstrong, but one couldn't cut with a broken blade. That blade had to be sharp and whole.

His thoughts scattered then rearranged themselves with their usual orderly precision. If he wanted the information she held in her head, he would need to be careful with her. He would need to be subtle and delicate. His usual methods would break her, which meant he would have to try a different approach.

Leaving her to his security team ran the risk of breaking her and, since that couldn't happen, the most logical thing was to deal with her himself.

Something coiled inside him, a certain sense of…anticipation. He ignored it the way he ignored most of his emotions, since there was absolutely no reason for it. No, handling her personally would be the best option all round and, though he couldn't really afford the time it would take for a more delicate interrogation, he'd make time.

The information she held was valuable. Michael Armstrong was powerful in England and did a lot of work for several Russian families, as well as some for French and Italian families that he was also in the process of dealing with.

Taking Armstrong down would be a blow and would effectively end their influence in England.

It would be worth it.

Are you sure that's the only reason you want to deal with her personally?

A sudden memory filled him, of the softness of her in his lap, her hair over his arm, her fingers clutching his shirt. She'd smelled sweetly of apples ripening in the sun, reminding him of summertime in the valley at his family's *palazzo*. Playing as a boy with Gabriella, before his mother had used him and changed everything.

'Mr de Santi,' Lucy said from behind him. 'What are—?'

'Drink your tea,' he interrupted, staring down at the empty fireplace, going over plans in his head. 'I will not have you fainting on me again.'

There was an annoyed silence behind him, then came the clink of a cup on a saucer.

He straightened and turned around.

She was holding the cup in her hand, sipping very pointedly on the tea, still looking highly irritated. A less perceptive man might have thought her fear had vanished, but he could see that it hadn't. Her knuckles had remained quite white and there was a certain darkness to her eyes.

Her father had locked her in a room in a basement with no windows when she wouldn't do what he told her…

Vincenzo felt something inside him shift and tighten. He'd asked her how often she refused to do her father's bidding and she'd said not very often. He could understand why if that panic attack was anything to go by. There were many ways to break a person's spirit, and leaving them alone locked up in the dark would certainly do it.

Except she wasn't quite broken, was she? There were glimmers of defiance and stubbornness in her hazel eyes, and certainly a broken woman would never have got up the gumption to escape her father in the first place.

Brave. He'd give her that at least.

'I'm drinking, see?' She lifted her cup again.

'Good.' He gave her a critical look, noting the colour in her cheeks. Probably she wouldn't faint again, and certainly not if he didn't threaten her with a cell. 'Are you going to give me the information I want?'

'About my father?'

'*Si.*'

Her gaze turned wary. 'I'm not sure. You might hand me over to the authorities if I do.'

A strange restlessness took hold of him and he wasn't sure if it was irritation or something else. 'I told you I would give you a week and I meant it.'

'A week of what?' She peered up at him from beneath her lowered brows, her wealth of dark hair curtaining her face again. 'A week of being in a cell?'

'There will be no cell, I've said so already.'

'But you didn't say what else there will be. I operate best with clear parameters, Mr de Santi.'

It was definitely irritation, he decided. 'Are you trying to bargain with me, *civetta?* Because I should tell you now that you are in no position to do so. You are only out of a cell at my pleasure and I can put you in one at any time.'

She continued to glare at him, but her hand was shaking a little, the tea in her cup rippling in response. And he had the oddest urge to put his own hand around hers to steady her. Or perhaps gather her into his arms again and hold her until she'd stopped shaking. Ridiculous. Where on earth were these urges coming from? He'd thought he'd put his protective instincts behind him a long time ago, especially when it came to women. Women were treacherous—more so than men, as he had good reason to know. His father had been ineffectual and weak, while it had been his mother who was the dangerous one. Small and exquisite and utterly merciless when it came to putting the de Santi name and its poisonous history before everything.

Even before her own son.

'But if you do that, I won't tell you anything,' Lucy pointed out. 'And you want me to tell you things, don't you?'

He gritted his teeth. 'I do not make bargains with prisoners.'

Lucy put her tea down, the saucer clattering on the table as she did so, tea spilling on her hand. She gave a little hiss of pain and he found himself instantly moving over to the table and reaching for one of the napkins on the tray, taking her small hand in his and dabbing the tea away gently.

She tried to pull her fingers from his, but he held on. He shouldn't give in to these urges and he knew it, but the hot liquid had burned her.

Because you are scaring her.

But he scared a lot of people. Why should scaring her feel so different?

'Let me go,' she murmured. 'It's just a little burn.'

He ignored her. Beside the tea and the plate of biscuits was a glass of water with ice in it, so he took one of the ice cubes out of the glass, wrapped the napkin around it and then pressed it gently against the burn on her hand.

'What do you want?' he heard himself ask, even though he'd told himself he wouldn't. That he definitely would enter into no negotiations with her.

Her hand trembled lightly in his grip and then, slowly, steadied.

'What do you mean?' she asked, her voice husky.

'You wanted a week of a normal life, you said. Is that the kind of thing you're talking about?' Her fingers were slender, her skin pale. Her hand looked very small in his. He couldn't think why he was tending to a tiny burn in this way. What was it about her that was making him do this? She wasn't beautiful and she wasn't charming. She didn't flutter her eyelashes and seduce him the way some women did. She didn't weep and she didn't scream. She was only scared. And wary. And guarded. Trying to stay in control even when he had all the power.

'You can't give me a normal life,' she said. 'You're going to hand me over to the authorities.'

He glanced up from her hand. 'You don't think you deserve to face justice for your crimes?'

Colour tinged her cheekbones and her gaze wavered. But he could read her very easily. She was ashamed and he thought that was genuine. Which meant she also thought she was guilty.

Your mother never thought she was guilty.

That was true, she hadn't. Not once. Not even when the police had dragged her away. It was a war, she'd kept telling him. And sometimes in a war there were casualties.

But it wasn't a war. Because if it had been, he'd have felt like a solider and not a murderer.

'No,' Lucy said, a little less certain now. 'I don't think that. I mean, I—'

'You have broken the law, Miss Armstrong. Numerous times.' Her hand in his pulled against his hold, but he didn't let her go, and he didn't look away. 'Do you think you should not have to answer for that?'

He could see her pulse beating very fast at the base of her throat, and as he watched she swallowed. She was radiating fear again and that angered him, though he didn't understand why. Because she had to fear him. She was supposed to.

As if she hasn't spent most her life being scared.

He didn't know if that was the case or why he should care even if it was. She wasn't any different from any other criminal. Her father might have forced her compliance by locking her in a dark basement, but that didn't change the fact that she had committed a crime.

Your mother used the same tactics on you, or had you forgotten?

No, that had been different. This little brown bird had only been locked in a room, fear keeping her in line, while his mother had used a far sharper tool. His mother had used his own love for her against him.

But Lucy didn't do what you did...

'I know I broke the law,' she said quietly. 'I know that. I hid his money for him and I helped him make more, and no I didn't do it legally. And I...' She stopped and pain flickered through her gaze. 'I know what he did with that money. But I was forced into it. I didn't *want* to do it, not any of it.' All the breath went out of her then and her shoulders slumped. 'I guess if that doesn't make a difference to you, then it doesn't. All I wanted was...a taste of what it would be like to be free.' Her voice had got soft, her fingers lax in his. She was staring down at her lap, all the defiance and mulishness leached out of her.

She looked defeated.

It should have satisfied him that he'd managed to break her, should have counted it as a win, and yet he didn't feel satisfied. And this didn't feel like winning.

This felt as if he'd destroyed something fragile and precious, and he didn't understand why. In fact, none of this made any sense. She was a criminal, regardless of whether she'd been forced into it or not, and as far as he was concerned she was guilty. He should have no feeling about her whatsoever. So why he should feel something tight in his chest and an anger in his soul he had no idea.

Perhaps it was only that he was annoyed with himself at his own clumsiness with her. He wasn't supposed to break her after all. He was supposed to be subtle. It wasn't his usual way—he preferred the direct approach, always—but he was going to have to try it at least, that much was clear. He didn't want her so terrified that she was useless to him, and if he carried on the way he was going that was exactly what she would be.

It was time for what the English called the 'softly, softly' approach.

'Give me your other hand,' he said quietly, and when she did so without protest he laid it over the top of the hand he was holding, keeping the napkin pressed to her skin.

Then he released her and straightened, looking down into her pale face. 'I can give you a week. No, it will not be complete freedom, but I can give you a small taste of it none the less. The price, though, remains the same. All the information you have on your father and your expertise to take down anyone associated with him.' He hesitated then said, 'If you do this, I will put in a good word with the authorities. Perhaps it will help make your sentence lighter.'

Her forehead creased, her gaze still wary. But he could see something glowing in it, something that looked a little like hope.

Poor *civetta*. She shouldn't hope. Hope was merely a drug to ease the pain and it only made everything worse when it ran out.

'Okay,' she said slowly. 'How do I know that you'll keep your word, though? That you won't put me in a cell or hand me over to the authorities the moment I give you anything?'

'You won't know.' He was not in the habit of sugar-coating anything and he didn't now. 'My word shall have to suffice.'

CHAPTER FOUR

LUCY TRIED NOT to be excited, but she couldn't help it as the small private jet touched down in Naples. She'd never left England before, had barely even left Cornwall, and now here she was in an entirely different country. It was almost overwhelming.

De Santi had dealt with customs technicalities with astonishing ease. He'd somehow produced a passport for her, even though she'd never had one, and she'd barely had a chance to look around after disembarking the aircraft before she found herself bundled into a helicopter. Then they were in the air again, flying over the sprawling city of Naples and then over the deep blue water of the ocean.

She couldn't drag her gaze from the sight of it. She didn't know where they were going—de Santi hadn't told her—and she didn't care. All that mattered was the wide blue of the water below her.

Finally, the sea. She'd listened to the waves at night in her bedroom in her Cornwall prison, but the house had no views and so she'd never seen the source of the sounds. Never seen such an expanse of blue.

She didn't know why it hypnotised her but it did.

Liar. You know exactly why you're letting it hypnotise you.

Okay, so, yes, she did. Staring at the sea was infinitely better than being conscious of the man sitting so closely beside her. Tall and powerful and utterly silent. He hadn't said a word the whole trip, at least not to her. He'd spent most of it on the phone talking to other people or looking intently at his laptop. A busy man, was Vincenzo de Santi, with a vast family business to run—since both his parents were now in prison and he had no other siblings, he had to run it alone—and a personal mission to take down as many of the European crime syndicates as he could.

Except somehow he'd found the time to whisk her away from London almost as soon as she'd agreed to pay his price for a week of freedom, and into Italy.

Once he put his mind to it, things certainly got done, she'd give him that, and if this was part of the taste of freedom he was offering her, then she was going to take it.

She wasn't sure what had changed his mind back in England, because it had seemed as if he was hell-bent on handing her to the authorities immediately. And she'd just about given up. She hadn't wanted to mention her mother—that was a private pain she wouldn't reveal to anyone—and so she'd waited for his judgment, feeling her defeat sweep through her.

And then he'd said that he would give her one week. It hadn't been exactly what she'd hoped for, but it was better than nothing. And it might be enough time for her to get him to change his mind about handing her over to the police. Because if he'd changed his mind once, then maybe he could change it again. If she was... persuasive enough.

You will have to be.

The thought was a warning and it made her afraid, so she ignored it. She was very good at ignoring the things that scared her, at seeing only what was right in front of her, and, since the sea was right in front of her now, that was where she looked.

Except she couldn't quite ignore the presence of the man beside her, no matter how hard she tried. His warmth was distracting, as was his intriguing scent. She'd never even thought a man could smell intriguing, but he did. It was disconcerting, too, that she could still feel how he'd held her hand when she'd burned herself on the tea, the heat of his skin on hers and then the cold press of the ice.

She'd been afraid of him then and she still was, yet she was drawn to him as well and she didn't understand how that could be. His strength and his power were both attractive and terrifying, as was the merciless way he looked at her, the cold ruthlessness of him, and yet how tightly he'd held her when she'd panicked.

No, she didn't understand how she could find him so fascinating and yet be so terrified of him at the same time. He was a panther, sunning himself on a rock, and she couldn't help wandering closer, wondering what it would be like to run her hands over his fur…

You're thinking of touching him now?

Lucy stared hard at the ocean. No, she definitely was *not* thinking of touching him. He was her enemy. He didn't care that she hadn't wanted to do any of the things her father had forced her into doing. In his eyes she was guilty and he would hand her over to the police once this week was done.

A creeping sense of cold threatened, only to vanish as the helicopter eventually soared over a big jewel of an island, all green with soaring cliffs and lots of expensive and very grand-looking mansions.

Ten minutes later they were coming in to land on a rolling flat green lawn that seemed to stretch to the edge of the ocean itself, an old, sprawling building constructed out of white stone sitting in the middle of it. There were lots of terraces and balconies, beautifully laid-out formal gardens and winding paths, the sun glittering off the sea beyond.

De Santi got out of the helicopter, ducking his head beneath the lazily turning rotors as he held the door open for her. She slipped out into the cool, salty air, the hot sun providing a delightful contrast. She wanted to just stand there and look around, but de Santi's fingers gripped her elbow and she was being guided along one of the paths and up some stone steps towards the big house.

A few people in uniform met them on a beautiful terrace that overlooked the sea, guards and probably housekeepers, all greeting de Santi in rapid Italian. He issued a few of what sounded like orders and then ushered her through some open double doors and into a large white room with big, deep sofas upholstered in a thick, textured white fabric. The floor was parquet and worn, as if centuries of feet had walked over it, the walls were white, with a few pieces of artwork here and there, decoratively displayed. A few antique pieces of furniture—shelves and a sideboard—also displayed various other artworks as well as being stuffed full of books and other knick-knacks.

The place was cool and quiet, and she could hear the sound of the sea. It might have bothered her, that sound, reminding her of things she didn't want to think about, but it felt different here. The air smelled different, was hotter, drier, and she could see the sea right there in front of her.

'Where are we?' she asked, as de Santi finished speaking with one of the uniformed women.

'Capri,' he said shortly. 'This is Villa de Santi, my family's holiday villa.'

She blinked, staring around the room. 'A holiday villa? This is…pretty amazing.'

'It's built on the remains of a historic Roman palace and has been in my family for generations. My family's actual estate is inland, near Naples, but I thought you would prefer to be near the sea.' He gestured towards the doors. 'You may wander at your leisure around the grounds, and don't worry, you'll be completely safe. My security is excellent.'

As if she'd needed any extra confirmation of his power… He had another house—no, estate—somewhere else on the mainland. But then, her research had confirmed that his resources were vast. An auction house in London was only the tip of the iceberg.

You will never escape him.

It was a strange thing to think when escaping him wasn't what she actually wanted, or at least not right now. She only wanted to change his mind about handing her over to the authorities.

Even though you deserve it?

No, she didn't. That was her fear talking. She ignored the thought. 'But only around the grounds,' she asked, to clarify. 'Not anywhere else?'

His eyes were dark as midnight and just as impenetrable. 'Of course not anywhere else. Your freedom is of a specific kind, *civetta*, and entirely at my pleasure.'

Not that she expected a different kind of answer. And this was already better than the house in Cornwall. Yes, she was still a prisoner, but at least she could see the sea. She could maybe even swim if she was lucky.

'Why do you call me that?' She frowned at him, distracted from swimming for a second. 'What does it mean? Is it "filthy prisoner" in Italian?'

An odd expression flickered over his face. 'No. It's nothing.'

'If it's nothing, then why say it?'

'It means "little owl".' He turned abruptly away. 'We will have a late dinner out on the terrace there. Martina will show you to your room and collect you when it's time to eat.' He was already moving towards the door. 'My staff do not speak English, so do not attempt to use them for any escape plans.'

She wasn't thinking of escape plans. 'Little owl?' she echoed blankly.

But he'd already vanished through the doorway.

How strange. Why would he call her that? Was she particularly owl-like? Perhaps it was an Italian term of disdain?

She had no more time to think of it, however, as one of the uniformed women bustled in, letting out a stream of musical Italian and gesturing at her.

Lucy followed her as the woman led her through the echoing halls of the house. It was a wonderful place, the ancient walls whitewashed, giving it a light and airy feel. Sometimes the flooring was smooth tiles, sometimes it was parquet, but there were always beautiful artworks on those whitewashed walls and richly coloured rugs on those floors. It was an intoxicating combination of simplicity and richness, the scent of the sea everywhere and the sound of the waves permeating the house. And she felt the hard knot inside her loosening a little further.

Martina showed her to a big room on the next floor, with that warm wood on the floor and those lovely white walls. Gauzy curtains hung over big windows that looked out over the intense blue of the sea, and there was a big, dark oak bedstead covered in white pillows and a white quilt against one wall. Through one door was a blue-tiled bathroom, and through another what looked like a dressing room.

Martina, still talking, disappeared then came back with a length of lustrous red fabric thrown over one arm. She laid it across the bed, gesturing emphatically at Lucy's dress. Lucy frowned then looked down at what she was wearing. 'What? I don't understand.'

Five minutes later it was apparent what Martina wanted, her firm hands briskly divesting Lucy of her handbag and then her dress. Shocked, Lucy could only stand there as Martina draped the red fabric around her shoulders, then tied it around her waist with a long red sash. The housekeeper stepped back, gave Lucy a satisfied look, then, holding Lucy's dress between one thumb and forefinger, as if it were something nasty she'd picked up after her dog, she went through the door and closed it behind her.

Well, that was interesting.

Lucy took a breath, looking down at herself again. It appeared that she was wrapped in the most gorgeous Chinese robe made out of thick, brilliant red silk and embroidered all over with gold dragons.

Clothes hadn't ever interested her, mainly because she had no one to dress for. She'd never cared about her appearance, didn't even think about it. But there was something…cool and delicious about the feeling of the silk against her skin.

Not sure what else to do, she poked around the room, picking various things up and examining them before putting them back down. And when she'd examined everything thoroughly, she went into the bathroom and examined that too.

The shower was vast and, since the journey had been a long one, she decided a shower was in order. Half an hour later, feeling better than she had in the past twenty-four hours, or even longer than that, she towelled herself dry and then considered her dirty underwear. She didn't really want to put it back on, so she didn't, wrapping herself up in the red silk dressing gown again and wandering out into the bedroom.

De Santi had mentioned something about a late dinner, which meant she had a bit of time beforehand, judging from the light outside the window. She stared at the door for a moment, then crossed over to it and gingerly tried the handle, expecting it to be locked.

It turned easily.

A wave of some emotion she couldn't identify washed through her. So she wasn't locked in, the way she was at home. He'd genuinely meant what he said when he'd told her she was free to wander.

Lucy stepped back from the door, the knot inside her almost coming undone. Then she turned and went over to the bed, got onto it and lay back, curling up on the white quilt. She felt tired, and now she knew the door wasn't locked the urge to get out and explore had left her for the moment. She closed her eyes instead, only for a second.

At least, it should have been a second.

When she opened her eyes again the light

had changed, long streaks of twilight painting the white walls in vivid pinks and reds and oranges. She lay there a second, getting her bearings, remembering where she was and what was happening. Then she slipped off the bed.

She felt hungry now and ready to eat, so she went into the bathroom to get her underwear, looking around to see if Martina had brought her dress back. But not only had the dress not been returned, her underwear had gone too.

Lucy frowned, wrapping the silk robe more tightly around her. Annoying. She felt under-dressed wearing only a dressing gown with nothing underneath it. There was nothing to be done about it, however, and, left with little choice, she eventually had to venture out of the bedroom wearing only the robe belted tightly at her waist.

The house was quiet and she encountered no one as she retraced the route Martina had led her on earlier, back into the big white lounge and out to the stone terrace again. It was beautiful in the twilight, the white stone glowing, the view framed by ancient olive trees, the table set for dinner.

Lucy stared at the table for a second, her chest feeling a little tight. There were candles and a white tablecloth and pretty wine glasses. It looked special. Not like a table set for a criminal and a prisoner.

Was this his doing? Or his staff? Did they know who she was? Perhaps they thought she was his girlfriend or his lover...

The tightness inside her twisted, making her feel hot. Disturbed, she turned away from the table and went to the edge of the terrace bounded by a low stone parapet. She sat down on it and looked out over the sea, taking in the amazing view.

There were so many boats, yachts with white sails and launches creating wakes, big super-yachts—floating palaces for the rich and famous—and smaller fishing boats. She imagined being on one and heading out to sea towards the setting sun, leaving everything behind to disappear over the edge of the horizon...

Maybe that would be her one day, finally escaping.

You think you really deserve to escape? Your mother didn't, so why should you?

Despite the view and the peace of the twilight, a chill whispered over her skin, curling through her soul.

Then a footstep sounded on the rough stone behind her, and she turned, thankful for the distraction, even though she knew who it was already.

It was him. De Santi. He'd obviously come through the French windows from the lounge area, and now he stopped as he approached the table, his dense black gaze flicking over her.

He'd removed his suit jacket, his white business shirt open at the neck, his sleeves rolled up. His skin was a smooth, dark olive, the muscles beneath it lean and sinewy. He should have looked casual and relaxed, but he didn't. Somehow the open shirt and rolled-up sleeves only served to make him appear even more ruthless, even more intimidating. The warrior angel ready to do battle.

He said nothing as he pulled a chair out and sat down, his movements loose and fluid. The setting sun bathed the almost medieval lines of his aristocratic face in gold, which should have softened him. Again, though, it was as if his presence rejected any attempts to mitigate it and instead the light simply illuminated even more strongly his dark ruthlessness.

He frightened her. Mesmerised her. Compelled her. She didn't know why. Yet again, she couldn't understand how a man could scare her and yet make her want to keep looking at him, as if she'd miss something if she glanced away.

Kathy, her mother, had been afraid of Lucy's father, she knew that much. It hadn't always been that way, Kathy had told her once. He had used to be a good man. But the years had turned him darker and he'd fallen in with bad people, and she had become afraid. Lucy had asked why they couldn't go away and live somewhere else. Her mother had only looked sadly at her and said, 'I love him.' As if that was explanation enough.

Lucy had never understood that. All it told her was if love was staying with someone who hurt you, then that was something very much to be avoided.

Not that love had any place here, with this man.

'Don't be like me,' her mother had said and yet here she was, inexplicably drawn to a dangerous man, and that scared her too.

He leaned back in his chair, his gaze still roving over her in a way that suggested he was hungry and she looked like something good to eat. It brought colour to her cheeks, made a strange, buzzing tension collect in the space between them and then go crackling over her skin like sparks.

Her cheeks were hot, her breathing oddly short, and the sound of her heartbeat echoed in her head. What was happening to her?

You know. You are more like your mother than you thought.

Lucy dragged her gaze away, back to the boats, an unfamiliar fluttering sensation in the pit of her stomach. No, that wasn't true. She didn't know enough about men to have any opinion on whether she was like her mother in that regard. Why would she? The only contact she'd had with them had been to be threatened by them. None of them had ever made her feel like…this.

'Sit at the table,' de Santi ordered coolly. 'Now, if you please.'

He didn't know what was wrong with him. Miss Lucy Armstrong was sitting on the stone parapet, the long twilight falling over her like gold dust, setting fire to the scarlet silk of the dressing gown and making the dragons embroidered on it dance. The colour made her skin look like porcelain and she must have done something to her hair because instead of the mat of dark brown, there was a wealth of glossy chestnut curls falling down her back. The gold in the embroidery of the robe picked up glints of gold in the depths of her hazel eyes and somehow, within the space of a few hours, this small, dull *civetta* had turned into something of a siren.

He couldn't take his eyes off her.

She slipped off the parapet she was sitting on, fumbling with the silk of the dressing gown as a bit caught on the rough stone. One side slipped a little off one shoulder, revealing a quantity of pale skin, and it was clear she wasn't aware of it because she didn't put the material back in place. Instead, she tied the belt tighter and came over to the table, pulling out the chair opposite him and sitting down. The movement made the fabric that should have covered her shoulder slip further down her arm, making it very apparent she was not wearing a bra.

Perhaps that was understandable. She had no

clothing except the ghastly dress she'd been wearing when she'd appeared in his office, and there had been no time for her to get any more. At least some of the afternoon he'd spent in his office had involved ordering her various items via one of his assistants. The villa didn't contain much in the way of female clothing or anything else, since he never brought any lovers here, or, indeed, anyone.

He was still puzzled as to why he'd brought her here. He'd told himself that it was because, although the de Santi *palazzo*, deep in the Campania countryside, was a much better place for a prisoner, being, as it was, built along the lines of a medieval *castello* rather than a palace and thus very secure, it was also a place that she might find frightening with its ancient walls and dark rooms. This villa was brighter, airier, and being on the sea with cliffs on one side made it easily defensible, not to mention the fact that Capri was an island and therefore it was less likely that she would escape.

All very good reasons and justifications for bringing her here, where he never brought anyone. And yet all he could think about was her voice telling him that she could hear the waves from her house in Cornwall and yet had never seen the sea.

You are getting soft, perhaps? Tired of the crusade?

No, of course not. And he would never tire. He needed her unafraid of him and willing to share the information in her head, that was all. And all of this was in aid of lulling those fears, making her relax, and who knew? Perhaps he could even get her to trust him?

She was staring down at her plate, her hands fussing with the silk of her robe as if she didn't know what to do with either them or herself. He made her uncomfortable, that much was clear. She'd blushed before, when he'd looked at her, and had glanced away, as if she'd felt the sudden tension between them too.

There is tension now?

Vincenzo gritted his teeth, trying to force the thought from his head as Martina and a couple of other staff members bustled over bearing quantities of food. Olives and bread and cheeses. Plates of fresh pasta with the excellent oil that she made from the olives in the gardens, and a tomato sauce to go with it. And a bottle of a very good red wine from the de Santi vineyards themselves.

The consummate professional, Martina arranged the food, poured the wine, then left, taking her staff with her.

Silence fell and he still couldn't take his gaze from her pale, uncovered shoulder.

Lucy reached for a piece of the fresh bread, but his patience was thinning, and when the robe slipped even more it ran out completely. He shoved back his chair and rose to his feet.

She looked up at him, her eyes wide and startled behind her glasses, and he knew he shouldn't do this, but he couldn't stop himself. He moved unhurriedly around the table to where she sat and paused beside her chair. Then gently he lifted the slipping fabric of the robe up and over her shoulder, covering her. A better man wouldn't have touched her, but he'd always known, deep down, that he wasn't a better man, so he allowed the backs of his fingers to brush over her bare skin. It was warm and even softer than the silk that covered it.

Her eyes went even wider, that vulnerable mouth of hers opening slightly as her breath caught. Colour flooded her cheeks, making her freckles turn pink, though he was more interested in the row of goosebumps that rose as he touched her.

It would be so easy to push that silk away instead of lifting it up, to uncover instead of conceal. Examine the curves he'd felt when she'd rested in his arms in his office, caress them, see if they were as satiny as the curve of her shoulder.

She was staring at him as if she'd never seen anything like him before in all her life, and though there was fear in her eyes there was also something else. Something that he'd seen in the eyes of other women who'd stared at him just like this one.

She was attracted to him, it was clear.

Perhaps you could use that to your advantage?

The thought streaked through his brain, bright and clear as a comet at midnight, but he dismissed it almost as soon as it had occurred to him. Those were his mother's tactics and he would never stoop to using those. Just as he would never indulge himself with her. Seduction was not and would never be one of his weapons. He was better than that. He had to be.

He turned away, ignoring the tight feeling in his body as he headed back to his chair. She was still staring at him, a bewildered look on her face.

It occurred to him, as he sat, that the slipping of her robe might have been purposeful, but one look at her expression told him it hadn't. She seemed to have no guile at all, which was definitely a rarity in a criminal.

'Why did you do that?' she asked, her voice slightly husky.

He ignored her. 'I have ordered clothing for you. It should arrive tomorrow. In the meantime you can continue to wear that robe.'

She frowned and he thought she might push, since he hadn't answered her question, but she didn't. Instead, she reached for the bread she'd been going to have before he'd interrupted her.

So, she was uncertain about this...chemistry between them, was she? It certainly seemed that way. She'd had no trouble speaking about other subjects, but she didn't want to push him on this. Interesting. Perhaps she was inexperienced. He wouldn't be surprised, given how her father had kept her prisoner.

'Why are you doing this?' she asked after a

moment, small fingers tearing apart the piece of bread. 'With the candles and the food. This beautiful house.'

'What do you mean?' He reached for his wine and picked up the glass, swirling the liquid around inside it.

That deep crease between her brows was back. 'I'm a prisoner. A criminal. Yet there are candles on the table.'

'I did tell you that you wouldn't have a cell.' He leaned back in his chair, sipping his wine, letting the flavour warm him, since nothing else did much these days; justice was a cold mistress. 'The candles were Martina's idea.'

They were not. They were his. He'd been concerned about the incipient darkness and wanted her to have some light, because he didn't want a repeat of her panic attack, that was all. But he didn't want to tell her that. It felt like giving away an advantage. 'You don't like them?'

'Oh, no, they're lovely. I just…' She stopped. Then lifted a shoulder as if the subject was one she'd lost interest in, and began layering some of the dip onto her bread with a knife. 'This smells very good,' she offered after a moment. 'I'm quite hungry.'

'That is obvious,' he observed dryly as she ate the piece of bread with small, precise bites then proceeded to get herself another. 'Are you ready to give me some information yet?'

She ate the other piece of bread then picked up her wine glass and took a sip. 'Is that why there are candles and nice food? You're hoping to bribe me into giving you what you want early?'

Irritation gathered inside him. It was true. He had promised a week. 'No,' he said shortly, even though he had a suspicion that was a lie as well. 'The candles and food are an added bonus. I do not bribe anyone, nor do I manipulate. You will give me what I want because I ask for it. Because we have made a bargain.'

She sipped again at her wine, frowning at him from behind the thick lenses of her glasses. 'Why is taking down my father so important to you? Did he do something to someone you know?'

'He's a criminal who has hurt others. He's a murderer, *civetta,* in case you didn't know. That's all the reason I need.'

An expression he couldn't read flickered over her face. 'Oh, I know what he is, believe me.

But is it him in particular? Or merely the fact that he's a criminal?' She regarded him curiously. 'Why don't you let the police deal with it?'

Was she really expecting him to tell her his reasons? To justify himself to someone like her? She'd be waiting a long time in that case, because he did not have to explain himself to anyone. Rumours followed him, naturally enough, but he didn't concern himself with them. The facts were his own and he gave them to no one.

No one else, for example, needed to know how his mother had seduced his father into the de Santi family 'business'. Or how she'd manipulated Vincenzo himself into doing the same thing, using his love for her against him.

He'd been her creature through and through. Her perfect boy, her heir. Her tool. There was a war, she'd told him, and their family had enemies that they had to defend themselves against. All lies. Lies he'd been too busy basking in her attention to see. Too busy being the chosen de Santi prince to care.

You knew. Deep down, somewhere inside, you always knew.

Some nights he lay awake in the dark, going over and over the things she'd told him to do, searching for signs he'd somehow missed. Signs he perhaps should have noticed—a cruel glint in her eye or a betraying curl to her lip. Something that would have told him that what she'd said about wars and soldiers and fighting were lies.

But there had been nothing. His mother had spent years perfecting her lies and he'd been sucked in completely. It was an evil he could never be free of and so all he could do was mitigate the damage by pursuing justice relentlessly.

No, he couldn't tell her that.

'I do let the police deal with it.' He kept his voice level and without emphasis. 'I give them the evidence they need, and they do the rest.'

'But isn't gathering the evidence their job?'

Annoyance gripped him. He didn't want her questioning him. 'They miss things. And they do not have the resources or the knowledge that I do. In some instances the police are corrupted by the very people they're trying to bring to justice.'

'You don't trust them, then?'

'No one can be trusted.'

'No one except you?'

Vincenzo realised he was holding his glass far too tightly and that if he held it any tighter the slender stem would snap. With a conscious effort he relaxed his fingers, staring across the table at the woman opposite.

There was nothing sly or knowing in her gaze, only curiosity. She wasn't goading him, it seemed; she genuinely wanted to know and obviously hadn't picked up on his irritation.

'You're not very polite, are you?' he observed casually, turning the conversation back on her.

Her eyes widened as if the statement had surprised her. 'Aren't I? Is asking questions wrong?'

'You are my prisoner, *civetta.* And a prisoner does not interrogate her captor.'

Colour tinged her cheekbones, giving her face a rosy flush. She really was quite pretty, now he thought about it. Which was not at all helpful.

'No, I suppose not.' She took another piece of bread. 'I just don't get to talk to people very often.'

'Why not?' he asked, since what was clearly

sauce for the gander could also be sauce for the goose.

She looked down at the piece of bread in her hands, tearing it once again into tiny pieces. And stayed silent. Her shoulders had hunched, her glossy hair a curtain over her face. The chestnut colour gleamed almost auburn in the fading twilight.

He was trespassing on painful subjects, it was clear, and no wonder. If her father had locked her in a dark basement, then what else had he done? But then, Vincenzo knew already. There were rumours about her, as there were about him; her father kept her well-guarded, deep in the English countryside. No, not just well-guarded. Her father had kept her prisoner.

The strange sensation in his chest that he'd felt earlier when he'd held her trembling body in his arms shifted again. A constriction.

He didn't like it and he knew he should let the subject alone, move on, even get up from the table and leave her here to finish her meal alone. Yet he didn't. Something compelled him to remain in his chair and to look at her all wrapped up in red silk, with her dark hair everywhere. Small and vulnerable and very, very alone.

'He kept you prisoner,' Vincenzo said, voicing his thoughts aloud to see her reaction. 'Didn't he?'

Her fingers shredded the bread to crumbs. 'I was too valuable to be let out, or at least that was what he told me. It was for my own protection. There were a lot of people who wanted to use me or kill me, and so I was safer in the house with the guards.'

The sensation shifted again, getting tighter.

'So you had no one at all you talked to? No friends? No family?'

'No. I had some online friends he didn't know about, but no one in real life. The only people I could speak with were him and my guards. But I didn't like speaking to the guards because they were...' She stopped.

But he could fill in the blanks. 'They frightened you?'

She lifted a shoulder, clearly not wanting to admit it.

'How long have you been a prisoner?' he asked, even though he shouldn't want to know, that it didn't matter. That being a prisoner was no less than what she deserved.

'Since I was seven.' Her hands rested beside her plate, still and tense.

'And how old are you now?'

'Twenty-two.'

Fifteen years she'd been her father's prisoner. Fifteen years.

He was aware that another sensation had joined the tightness in his chest, something hot that felt like anger, though it couldn't have been. Because she was a criminal and needed to face justice, and it seemed that she'd served fifteen years of equivalent jail time already. A just sentence. Especially when she would have been committing even more crimes in that time.

She has been alone all her life. Like you have been alone.

No, it was not the same. And he wasn't alone. He had his staff and business colleagues, and anyway, he didn't need anyone. The path he'd chosen for himself was one he could only walk himself. No one else could walk beside him and he'd known that when he'd chosen it.

You are serving a sentence just like her.

He ignored that thought. His own guilt had nothing to do with this and he didn't need that contributing to the already tangled knot of emotions inside him. Emotions that he would have told himself even a day ago he no longer felt.

He was a fool. He shouldn't be sitting here talking to her about her life. He had better things to be doing with his time.

Vincenzo put his glass down on the table with a click. 'None of that matters, of course. You are guilty, Miss Armstrong. And at the end of the week you will pay for your crimes.'

CHAPTER FIVE

LUCY COULD HEAR the certainty in his deep, cool voice and it sent yet more chills through her. Clearly he'd finished making conversation. And he had been making conversation, that was obvious.

She shouldn't have asked him all those questions. She'd only been...curious about him and why this justice crusade he was on was so important, and she shouldn't have been. Curiosity had always got her into trouble and she shouldn't indulge it.

Sadly, he hadn't given her reasons for his crusade, though that was understandable. As he'd said, a prisoner didn't interrogate her captor.

And he's right that you should pay. You are *guilty.*

A shiver chased over her skin. If she was guilty of anything, it was of not standing up to her father. Of cowardice. Except cowardice didn't deserve a jail term.

However, he certainly seemed to think it did. She had to change his mind somehow, convince him to let her go.

Incorruptible, they said of him, but, as her father liked to remind her, every man had his price.

What was Vincenzo de Santi's?

Slowly she raised her head and looked at him, her heart thudding strangely in her chest as she met his inky gaze.

He was leaning back in his chair, the casual arrogance he carried around with him everywhere he went even more palpable. The menace that gathered like a cloak at his back even stronger. He was dark and he was dangerous and yes, she was frightened.

But she was always frightened. Of everything. She'd been frightened since she'd been seven years old and her mother had died right in front of her eyes.

Yet Kathy hadn't let fear of her husband stop her from protecting her daughter. She'd been brave; why couldn't Lucy follow her example?

You have other weapons at your disposal, remember?

She frowned, trying to puzzle the thought out, because what other weapon could there be?

He is a man and you are a woman...

A flash of heat seared her skin, passing over her so fast she barely had time to draw a breath before she could feel burning in her cheeks. Burning everywhere.

Because he *was* a man and the way he'd looked at her earlier, unable to tear his gaze from her bare shoulder, had been very much the way a man a looked at a woman. He'd been... hungry...

The heat deepened. She'd never thought of having a lover, had never liked the idea of getting that close to a man, not after what her father had done to her mother.

She had never regretted her decision. She didn't think of the future beyond her mother's promise. Have a life, Kathy had told her, but Lucy didn't let herself think about what that life would contain, because it was only the escape that mattered.

But if she *had* thought about it, a man wouldn't have featured anywhere. Yet a part of her now wondered if this would have been easier if she'd managed to find herself a lover.

Not that her father had given her any opportunity to find one, but still. Maybe if she had she might know what to do, how to use de Santi's definite hunger to her advantage.

Because she could, couldn't she? This could be a way for her to take control, to get some power for herself. She could offer herself in return for her freedom. Some women did that, didn't they?

Of course, he could just take what he wanted from her whether she let him or not, but it was unlikely that he'd force himself on her physically the way some men did. Surely a man who'd held her in his arms while she'd been paralyzed with fear, who'd tended to her burn, wouldn't be physically violent, not the way her father had been. De Santi was a much more controlled man.

Her heartbeat had speeded up, her breathing becoming unsteady. He watched her as if he could read every thought in her head and knew exactly what she was planning, his eyes gleaming obsidian black in the night.

Was she really contemplating using her sexuality to get what she wanted? Hoping that she could earn her freedom that way? Because what did she know of seduction? Nothing. She was a virgin in every way there was, while he was a man of no doubt infinite experience. Plus, she was a terrible liar and an even worse actress. She wouldn't be able to pretend something she didn't feel.

Are you sure you don't feel it?

Her heart beat harder, fear like a fist slowly closing inside her. Yet…not only fear. Or maybe it was a different kind of fear, because this type didn't feel bad. No, it felt…like a fine electrical current, sparking over her skin, sizzling wherever it touched.

She wasn't a seductress. She didn't know how to do this with any subtlety or grace. Direct was the only approach she knew. So she took another sip of wine—it was more of a gulp really—and put down her glass. Then she made herself hold his dark gaze and put one hand on the knot of her sash. 'Are you sure I can't get you to change your mind? Perhaps there's something I can give you that might help.'

Then she pulled the sash and let her robe fall open.

The last rays of the sun had gone, leaving only a deepening purple darkness that crept over everything. The candles flickered and danced, catching the gleam of his ink-black eyes as he stared at her. A breeze moved over her skin, making goosebumps rise on the thin strip of flesh she'd bared. Though that could have been the heat of his gaze.

She didn't look away, conscious that it wasn't only fear inside her now, but something more complicated than that. Like a delicate fabric shot through with threads of silver and gold, her fear had other things woven through it, emotions she'd barely felt before. A breathless excitement. The tight coil of anticipation. A nagging ache right down low inside her, between her thighs.

'What are you doing, *civetta?*' The question sounded idle, as if she'd done something mildly curious that he was puzzled about. But there was nothing idle about the tension that gathered around his powerful form. He was very still, the panther about to pounce.

Her pulse was loud in her ears and she wasn't sure if this was a good idea, but she'd taken this step and there was nothing to do but go on with it.

'Isn't it obvious? I undid my robe.'

'I can see that. Are you hot, perhaps?'

Had he misunderstood her? Were her seduction skills that bad? Or was he deliberately misreading the situation? Probably deliberately misreading it, surely?

'I'm not hot. I would very much like not to be handed over to the police at the end of the week and I thought that perhaps I could…change your mind.'

She wanted to cover herself, conscious of how the flickering candlelight was illuminating the bare curve of one breast. It wasn't the same as being wholly naked, but she'd never even been partially naked in front of anyone, let alone a man she was afraid of. A man she'd only known a matter of hours. A stranger.

It made her feel very vulnerable. But she was tired of feeling alone and powerless. Tired of feeling afraid all the time and so she didn't look away. He might be frightening, yet she refused to give in to her fear.

His face remained unreadable, his eyes glittering. 'Are you trying to manipulate me with sex, Miss Armstrong? Because I should warn you now, I don't respond well to it.'

She shivered slightly at the chill in the words.

Clearly she was on dangerous ground. 'I… didn't intend it that way, no.'

'Then what did you intend? Do you think I'm a man who would be swayed by such things?'

The urge to cover herself returned, stronger this time as his gaze slid slowly down her body, dipping to where her robe opened. But she didn't move. She had the distinct impression that he was not…unaffected.

'I don't know,' she said, her voice hoarse. 'Are you?'

He lifted his gaze to hers again, unhurried. 'No. I am not. Especially when the woman concerned is afraid of me and doesn't want me.'

A little shock went through her. Did she want him? She'd never wanted anyone before, so how would she know? Was it possible to want someone you were afraid of?

But it's not just fear that you feel for him.

The shock deepened as she stared at him in the darkness, the light from the candles flickering over his strong features, touching on the harsh planes and angles of his face, shadowing the deeper darkness of his eyes and the hollow of his throat…

She wanted to tell him that she didn't think

it was only fear that she felt for him, but her hesitation must have given her away, because he moved abruptly, shoving back his chair with some force. He didn't say anything, merely gave her one last, fierce look that she couldn't interpret, then turned and left her sitting there in the dark, with her robe open and the shock getting deeper and wider inside her.

Vincenzo didn't know what to do. He was furious, both with himself for wanting what he shouldn't, and with Miss Lucy Armstrong for offering something he couldn't help wanting and in such a way as to ensure he could never take it.

Not only was she a criminal whose crimes had hurt people, but she'd also used her body as a bargaining chip. She'd said that she hadn't meant it that way, yet he felt manipulated all the same.

'Ask Gabriella out, Vincenzo,' his mother had told him all those years ago. *'Go to the cinema and have some dessert afterwards. Get her to tell you what her father's movements are, especially whether he's planning on returning home after the play on Friday night or whether*

he's going out. And if he's going out, we need to know where.'

He'd been older then, eighteen, and starting to suspect that his beloved mother's casual requests were never as casual as they seemed, and so of course he asked why this was necessary. Why he couldn't just enjoy a date with his childhood friend and whom he was beginning to have feelings for.

'Oh, it's just some family business, my handsome boy. Nothing to be concerned about. I like to keep tabs on people. You know that.'

And she'd given him the most radiant smile, and he'd forgotten his doubts and suspicions. All he'd wanted was to make his mother happy.

Of course it was just business. Of course it was nothing to be concerned about.

So he'd taken Gabriella out and casually asked her about her father, then later relayed the information to his mother. And two days later, Gabriella's father had died in a hit. No one knew which family had been responsible, but Vincenzo had known. And so had Gabriella.

She'd realised Vincenzo had betrayed her. That he was the one who'd got her beloved father killed and that he'd made her complicit in it too. That the downfall of her own family was her fault, and all because a childhood friend had asked her a few seemingly simple questions.

He'd never forgotten the sound of Gabriella's devastated voice ringing in his ears as she'd called him the next day, confronting him with what he'd done, full of fury and grief. Nothing he could say would have made it better, because he knew what he'd done just as she had.

Afterwards, he'd gone to his mother as the shock of the assassination of a major player echoed through the crime families of Europe. She'd merely shrugged her shoulders.

'As I told you, Vincenzo. It's just business. So I would get used to it if I were you.'

She'd given him another of those radiant smiles.

'If you want to remain part of this family, that is, which I'm sure you do. You've already done so much for us as it is...'

But he knew he would never get used to it, just as he knew what his mother had issued with that lovely smile was a threat. She'd never done that before, but he understood what it was all the same. A reminder of his own actions, that he wasn't innocent and never would be, and that what she gave she could also take away.

It was in that moment that he'd realised what he was to her: not a son but a tool to build her empire. She'd never loved him. He'd never been her handsome boy. He'd been spoiled and pampered and paid attention to, but only so she could turn him into her creature. The way his father had always been her creature.

So that night he'd pretended to be her loving son, her yes-man, just as he always had. Then he'd gathered what information he could about her activities and sent it to the police.

Two days later she and his father had been arrested, justice served.

But he would never again let himself be used the way his mother had used him. Never let his own feelings blind him to the truth. He would always listen to his conscience and never let his emotions sway him.

He would always do what was right, and sleeping with the little *civetta* because she offered, and because he wanted her, was wrong.

And he did want her. And he was furious about it.

He kept away from her the following day, to

give her some distance and to give his recalcitrant body some time to rethink its choices. There were matters that needed his attention anyway. Her father was trying to contact him, no doubt to offer terms for her return, and Vincenzo was almost tempted to see what the man would say, but then, he knew anyway. Armstrong only used either bribery or threats, neither of which would work on Vincenzo. He couldn't take his daughter by force, either, since he didn't have the resources to touch her on Capri, not without getting allies at least, and that would take time.

Regardless, Vincenzo could afford to wait. He'd let Armstrong suffer for the next week, or for however long it took Lucy to give him the information he wanted.

So he closeted himself in his office in the villa, dealing with the thousand and one things he had to deal with, while his brain kept replaying the memory of her sitting in the dusk with her robe half-open, the shadowed curves of her body a temptation he hadn't envisaged. The rounded shape of one breast—fuller than he'd expected, given how small she was—and the graceful arc of one hip. Her skin had been such a pretty pink, highlighted by the red silk she wore, and his desire had risen, thick and hot. Shocking in its intensity.

He wouldn't have taken her even if she had wanted him, but he knew that she didn't. Her eyes behind the shelter of her glasses had been very wary, the fear glittering greenly in their depths.

It had angered him, that fear. His desire angered him. Her offer had angered him.

Everything had angered him and so he'd pushed himself to his feet and left before he did something he regretted, such as reaching for her and dragging her across the table and burying that anger between her thighs.

Yet even immersing himself in business didn't help. He felt restless and unable to concentrate, her presence an itch he couldn't scratch, and he was further annoyed that he had to wait until the week had ended before he'd get the information he needed to take down her father.

He would have gone back to the de Santi estate himself and left her here if he could have. But he couldn't. Even though his security was impregnable, he didn't want to leave anything to chance. He had to be here to keep an eye on her.

She might try to manipulate him again, of course, but if she was hoping that he'd change his mind about her she was mistaken. He would not be changing his mind. She needed to answer for her crimes so justice would be served.

The thought hardened his resolve, though it did nothing for the restlessness that coiled through him as the day progressed into night. He stayed in his office till midnight, and only then did he leave, stalking back to his bedroom in search of sleep.

He didn't find it, however, and after several hours of lying there, staring at the ceiling, he admitted defeat and slid out of bed, pulling on some jeans and prowling downstairs to the salon that led out onto the big terrace.

It felt hot and airless, so he went to the double doors and pushed them open, allowing the salt-soaked night air and moonlight to pour in. He stood in the doorway a minute and took a deep breath, trying to find his usual clarity of purpose, the bone-deep knowledge that what he was doing was right and necessary.

He couldn't allow himself to be distracted from it by an inconvenient attraction to the worst possible woman. He wouldn't. He must keep on with his crusade, right the wrongs his family had perpetrated over the centuries, that his mother had carried into this century too. It would end with him, that was certain.

Behind him came the sound of a soft footstep and a whisper of an indrawn breath, and he was turning, instantly on his guard. He normally had a weapon with him, but since the villa was well-protected he hadn't bothered with one to-night.

Not that he needed one.

A small figure stood in the darkness near the door to the hall. There was enough moon-light for him to see golden dragons gleaming on red silk and the gloss of dark curls, of light reflected off the round discs of her glasses. The sweet scent of apples reached him and he felt himself go still, his entire body tightening in anticipation.

You're getting ahead of yourself. She didn't want you, remember?

He remembered. She'd been made of fear, not desire.

'I'm sorry,' she murmured in her husky voice. 'I didn't know you were here. I'll go if you—'

'What are you doing up, *civetta*?' He shouldn't

ask. He should leave her the way he'd left her the night before. Yet he didn't move.

'I…couldn't sleep.'

'Why not?'

'I don't know.' She shifted on her feet, silk rustling, sounding uncertain and nervous. 'I was just…restless.'

As he was restless.

Perhaps it's for the same reason?

Perhaps. But again, last night, he hadn't seen desire in her when she'd opened her robe. Only uneasiness and nerves.

You could be wrong.

A thread of heat wound its way through him and he found himself wanting to see her face, see what expression was in her hazel eyes.

'Come here.' He had to put some effort into not making it sound like an order, but he managed it. Part of him wanted to know if she would come if it wasn't a command. If she would come because she wanted to.

She hesitated, but only for a moment, and then she came slowly towards him, the moonlight moving over glorious red silk, dark curls, and pale skin.

He could see her face now as she stopped a

few feet from him, laid bare in the light coming from behind his back. The moon had bleached all the colour from her cheeks, turning her eyes very dark. With the lenses of her glasses reflecting the light, she looked even more owlish than she normally did.

The night before when he'd told her that she didn't want him she hadn't denied it. She'd simply looked at him as if wanting him hadn't entered her head, even though she'd been fully prepared to offer him sex. And he couldn't lie to himself. The fact that she hadn't wanted him had angered him too.

'Yes?' The word was tentative, her gaze full of familiar wariness.

'Perhaps you can't sleep for the same reason I can't,' he said.

'I...' She stopped, and her hands moved nervously to the sash of her robe, touching it before falling away again. 'What reason would that be?'

He might have thought she was deliberately misunderstanding him if he hadn't known already that she had no guile whatsoever. But, as he was learning, she wasn't like his mother; her response had the ring of truth to it. She genu-

inely didn't know. Which meant that she had
no sexual thoughts about him at all, or she was
so desperately inexperienced she didn't recog-
nise them.

*Does it matter? You're not going to take her
anyway.*

It didn't matter. And of course he wasn't.

'Were you thinking of me?' he asked, not
moving, not taking his gaze from hers.

Even in the moonlight he saw the flush rise
in her cheeks.

'Yes,' she admitted hesitantly.

The confession hit him like a jolt of electricity, unexpected and raw as a lightning strike,
making his hands curl into fists at his sides.

'Why?' This time he couldn't make it sound
like anything less than a demand.

'I don't know. I can't work it out. I'm…afraid
of you. And yet I can't stop thinking about you.'
The blush in her cheeks got even deeper. 'That
was too honest, wasn't it?'

But that was what she was, wasn't it? Too
honest. And in ways he was only now beginning to understand. Honesty had been so rare
in his life, he barely recognised it. Yet there
was more to her than simple honesty. She was

also wary and guarded, as if she didn't know what parts of herself she should be protecting.

He wasn't sure why that was, but one thing he did know. He didn't want her to be afraid of him. Thinking of him, yes. Scared, no.

He held her gaze. 'Honesty is rare these days and it is precious. Never apologise for it.'

She blinked, then her gaze dropped from his, down to his chest, which was bare, since he hadn't bothered with a shirt. And stayed there a second before she looked away, nervously fiddling with the knot of her sash.

She wasn't a seductress, he knew that already, and he knew, too, with sudden insight, that she would never have offered him what she had if she hadn't on some level been attracted to him. It simply wouldn't have occurred to her.

But she was attracted to him. Her problem was that she didn't know what it was, because she had no experience. She had no experience of anything at all.

'And are you afraid now?' He searched her vulnerable face. 'Afraid of me?'

Her fingers pulled at her sash. 'Yes.' She said the word tentatively, as if she wasn't sure whether she should reveal it to him or not.

That wasn't what he wanted, not here, not now. She'd been afraid for a long time and right now he didn't want her to be. Just as he didn't want to be only one more man who scared her.

Vincenzo didn't stop to question himself. He merely reached out and took one of her nervous hands in his and slowly drew it towards him. She tensed, looking up at him, her eyes widening. But she didn't pull away, allowing him to place that small hand palm down on his bare chest. Then he put his own over the top of it, holding it there.

The hiss of her indrawn breath echoed in the still darkness, her touch on his skin as warm as sunshine resting on him. Her eyes were wide, that soft, vulnerable mouth open.

'And are you afraid now?' he asked quietly.

CHAPTER SIX

LUCY WANTED TO tell him that she wasn't afraid. But she was. She was terrified.

Of the smooth, oiled silk of his skin. Of the heat of his body. Of all the hard muscle she could see clearly etched in sharp, carved lines all over his torso. Of the strength and power that hummed through him like electricity through a high-tension wire.

His eyes were the night itself beyond the terrace and his face was all brutal beauty and ferocity, a combination that mesmerised her.

She'd told the truth. She'd come downstairs, restless and unable to sleep, because she'd been thinking of him. She'd been thinking of him all day and she didn't know how to stop.

The words he'd said to her the night before kept revolving in her head, taking up space. Making her angry that he would dare to tell her what her own emotions were and yet also making her examine those emotions. Examine the fear that lived inside her and had done so ever since her mother had died.

Yes, she was afraid of him, but it was such a complex fear. And she'd never wanted anyone before, had never thought about physical hunger that wasn't for food. Had never felt drawn to anyone at the same time as she was afraid of them. It made her think of her mother and how afraid she'd been of Lucy's father. Yet she'd stayed with him all the same.

Love, that had been the issue, though, Lucy was sure.

And she didn't love Vincenzo.

The whole day she'd done her best to do her usual thing, which was to pay attention only to the moment as she'd explored the villa, to never think about anything else. Yet it gradually became clear to her as the day went on that she wasn't just exploring the villa. She was also looking for him. Wanting to see him, talk to him. Ask him how he knew that she didn't want him, because she wasn't sure that was the case.

She didn't think it was the case now as he held her hand to his powerful chest, the inky black of his gaze holding hers. She wanted… She didn't know what she wanted. Not love, that was for sure. In fact, she'd never want that, but sex? Maybe.

Sex wasn't a mystery to anyone with an internet connection and she'd looked up various things. It had all looked faintly ridiculous and like nothing she'd ever want to participate in, but what she'd seen on her computer screen had nothing to do with the reality of Vincenzo de Santi, half-naked, in the middle of the night in a villa on Capri, watching her with heat in those black eyes.

There was nothing ridiculous about him. Nothing ridiculous about the heat inside her either.

Why isn't he simply taking you?

A good question. Powerful men took what they wanted, as she knew all too well, but he wasn't taking her. He hadn't the night before either, even though she'd offered herself to him. In fact, he'd got up and left rather than reach for her, and that only added a layer to the complex puzzle he was turning out to be.

An incorruptible man, yet not a man without hungers. A man with a strong moral code who stuck by that morality regardless of what he might want for himself.

He is not your father. You don't have to be afraid of him.

Lucy swallowed, her mouth dry. It was true. He *wasn't* anything like her dad. And she wasn't anything like her mum. Once she'd been fearless like her. Brave and inquisitive and curious, too. But that had been before those things had led to her mother's death, so these days she locked them away. Fear kept her safe, after all.

Yet last night she'd realised that she was tired of being afraid, and now she realised something else. She was tired of being afraid of Vincenzo. The frightened little girl she'd spent so many years being wanted to pull her hand away and run to the safety of her bedroom. But the woman who'd spent a day near the sea, who'd smelled the salt and watched the boats, who'd opened her robe and offered herself to a dangerous man, didn't want to leave. Right now there was a fascinating and beautiful panther in front of her. And she was ruffling his fur and nothing bad was happening. He wasn't being violent. He wasn't hurting her. He was only holding her hand to his chest. And she was so very curious about what would happen if she stroked him…

You're not afraid of him. You're afraid of yourself, of what you want...

She took a breath, feeling something shift and turn inside her, a hunger of her own that she'd ignored. A hunger that there was no way of satisfying, held prisoner as she was in her father's house. So she'd ignored it, shoved it away. Forced it down.

But it was still there. And it was strong. And yes, it scared her.

'Yes,' she whispered and she felt him tense, the expression in his eyes changing, as if that wasn't the answer he wanted. 'Does it matter?'

A muscle in his jaw leapt. 'Of course it matters.'

'Why? Isn't my being afraid what you want?'

His hold remained gentle on her hand, but his gaze was not gentle in the slightest. 'No. You've been afraid for too long, *civetta*, and I don't want that for you. Not now. Not here. Not with me.'

She wanted to ask him what made now different. But that was a rabbit hole she didn't want to go down, not with her hand on his warm chest and the hunger inside that kept on getting wider, getting deeper. That she was afraid of, because it felt bottomless. It felt as if it would swallow her whole.

'I don't think it's you,' she said. 'I think… I'm afraid of myself.'

'Oh?' His thumb moved on the back of her hand, a gentle caress that sent sparks glittering all over her skin.

'I'm afraid of what I want.' A shake was beginning in the pit of her stomach, a tremor like a small earthquake. 'I think I'm more afraid of that than I am of you.'

Tension was gathering in him, but his hold on her hand remained gentle. She could pull away at any moment. 'And what is it that you want, *civetta?*'

He knew, she could see it in his eyes. But he wanted her to say it.

You can't be so afraid all the time. You only have a week. You only have now. Tell him and let him give it to you. This chance won't come again.

And he would give it to her. He wanted to.

Lucy took a slow, silent breath and made herself hold his gaze. 'You were wrong last night.' Her voice was little more than a hoarse whisper in the night. 'I do want you. And I spent all today exploring the villa, but I think… I wasn't exploring. I was searching.' She tried to moisten her dry mouth. 'I was searching for you and I couldn't find you.'

The moon was behind him, glossing his black hair and throwing his face into shadow. But that shadow couldn't hide the flare of heat that leapt in his eyes. 'Well,' he murmured, and this time his voice wasn't cold or casual, 'you have found me.'

The tremble became deeper, wider, the tremor turning into an earthquake. 'Yes,' she said, unable to think of anything else to say.

His thumb moved on the back of her hand again. 'And now you have found me, what are you going to do with me?'

'I don't know.' Her pulse was getting louder and louder in her ears. 'I don't know anything. I've never… I haven't…' The hunger inside her felt too big to contain and she knew if it got any bigger it would shatter her. But she had no experience of this, had no idea what she should be doing. She could hide millions of dollars in offshore tax havens, make them disappear completely, but she had no idea how to touch a man. 'Please…' That one word was a request, a plea, an order. Encompassing everything she didn't know how to say.

An expression she couldn't read rippled over his face, then it was gone, and he was looking at her, the blackness of his eyes becoming the entire world. He raised her hand from his chest and brought her palm to his mouth, pressing a kiss to it.

She gasped, the feeling of his lips against her skin like a hot coal being held there.

Then, keeping her hand in his, he reached out with the other and slowly threaded his fingers in her hair, cradling the back of her head, drawing her closer. She was shivering now, but she didn't pull away; she didn't think she could even move.

And when he lowered his head and that burning mouth covered hers all thoughts of moving vanished entirely. Every thought vanished entirely.

His kiss had taken them all, including her fear.

Something opened inside her like a flower opening for the sun, a knowledge that had been sitting in her soul all this time. That she'd been waiting for this moment her entire life. Waiting for him. She was Sleeping Beauty and he was the prince waking her from sleep, and now he was here there was nothing to be afraid of. Nothing at all.

The trembling took over as he kissed her and so did her need, and her mouth was opening beneath his as if she knew what to do already, letting in his taste and his heat. It felt as if the kiss was a match, igniting her, and now she was burning so hot it felt as though the flame would never go out.

She hadn't meant to deepen the kiss, because he'd started off so gentle, but now his tongue was exploring the inside of her mouth, tasting her with more demand, and she didn't know how to hold back. She followed his lead, tasting him in return, taking in the rich, spicy flavour of him and letting it settle down into her bones. Into her heart.

One of her hands was still held in his, pressed hard to his chest, but she wanted more than that. More than his beautiful mouth talking to her in a language made of teasing kisses, gentle nips, and coaxing licks. She wanted the heat of that powerful body against hers, wanted to press herself to his velvet skin, explore what he felt like, because she didn't know and the lack of that knowledge was an ache inside her.

She moved closer, put her other hand on his chest, glorying in the heat of his body and the feeling of strength. It didn't frighten her, not any more. She knew to the depths of her soul that he would never use that strength to harm her, not the way her father did, and now all she wanted was to explore that strength. Touch that power. Have it turned on her to bring pleasure, not pain.

He released her hand and his arms were around her, pulling her close so she was where she wanted to be, pressed up against him. His mouth had turned hot on hers, the kiss more demanding, and yet even now expertly controlled. More and yet not more than she could handle.

She wanted to handle it though. Because, now she wasn't afraid, all that was left inside her was strength.

His hands slid from her hair down her back and suddenly she was lifted in his arms, held tight to his chest as he crossed the room to one of the long, low sofas. He put her on the cushions, sitting her upright, then came down on his knees in front of her.

She reached for him but he only took her hands in his, turning them palm up and pressing a kiss on each one. Then he put them on the couch and held them there, his gaze fierce on hers. 'Keep them there,' he ordered, his voice full of dark heat. 'Let me give you this, *civetta*. Let me show you how good I can make you feel.'

Lucy took an unsteady breath, shivering all over, held fast by the fierce, hungry look in his eyes. She nodded.

He took his hands away from hers then put them on her knees, easing them apart so he could kneel between them. She took another trembling breath as he came closer, his lean hips between her thighs, his bare chest inches away. He was so tall that, even sitting, she was barely at eye level with him, the breadth of his shoulders blocking out the night behind him.

Calmly he took her chin in one hand, holding her still as he leaned down and kissed her again, his lips hot, the kiss so achingly sweet that she moaned. He deepened it, his tongue dipping inside her mouth, and as he did so she felt his fingers slide beneath the silk of her robe.

Clothes had arrived for her that afternoon,

but she hadn't gone through them all, and she hadn't been bothered to find any nightgowns or pyjamas. She'd gone to bed naked and now he knew that too, his fingers burning like a brand on the sensitive skin of her shoulder as he stroked her.

It felt so good that she trembled harder, shivering all over as his grip on her chin loosened and his fingers spread out along the side of her jaw, cupping it, his thumb stroking along her skin as he kissed her deeper. With his other hand he eased the silk of her robe aside, the tips of his fingers brushing down her side and lightly following the curve of her bare breast.

Lucy shuddered, the tips of her nipples abruptly achingly sensitive. She wanted him to touch them, but he didn't. He only caressed her side and then traced circles over her skin, teasing her, maddening her. His mouth left hers and trailed down the side of her neck, leaving kisses like fallen stars and nips like hot sparks. Making her shake, her fingers curling into the material of the sofa cushions, holding on tight.

She wanted more, so much more, but he was going so slowly and being so careful, and he didn't need to. She wasn't afraid, not of him. Not any more.

'Please, Vincenzo.' She'd never called him that to his face before, but it felt right on her tongue. It felt perfect. 'Please... I w-want—'

'Patience,' he murmured against her skin, kissing down between her breasts as his hands caressed her hips and thighs. 'I know what you want and I'll give it to you, I promise. But anticipation will make it sweeter. And besides, I want to savour you.'

He did? Was she worth savouring? Her mother had died protecting her and sometimes, in her lowest moments, she wondered if her mother's sacrifice had really been worth it. Because after Kathy had died her only value lay in what she did for her father, her analytical brain and her facility with numbers. And it was a value predicated on hurting others...

So no, sometimes she didn't think she'd been worth saving. But now here was Vincenzo, telling her that he wanted to savour her, making her feel almost as if she had been worth it after all...

Inexplicable tears collected behind her lids, but she blinked them back fiercely. She wasn't going to cry, not while he was doing this to her. And she wasn't going to protest, either. Not while he was making her feel so good. She didn't want to be sad with him, she only wanted this feeling, this pleasure to never end. Because she'd never had it before. There were so many things she'd never had before and all because of him.

He kissed down her stomach, his hands stroking, making the sweet ache between her thighs become more acute, more demanding, sending delicious chills everywhere. Then he was pushing her thighs wider, his mouth moving lower, and she found herself arching back, ready for anything he might give her. It would only be good, surely.

His fingers stroked her inner thighs, his mouth finding the hot, wet centre of her. Exploring gently, tasting lightly, and she was shaking so hard she thought she might come apart, her breathing loud, her heartbeat louder.

An ocean of pleasure rose up around her, hot and liquid like honey, drowning her, but she didn't care. She wanted to drown. She never wanted to come up for air again.

His hands slid beneath her thighs, drawing

her close to the edge of the sofa, and she leaned back, gasping as he lifted her leg and draped it over one powerful shoulder, allowing him greater access, and then his mouth was back on her, tasting her deep inside as his hands caressed her.

There were lights behind her eyes, falling stars and supernovas, galaxies glittering, the end of the world approaching. And she had a front-row seat.

Until even that was lost as the pleasure took everything from her, leaving her with nothing, not even her name. But it wasn't frightening. She threw herself into it, happy to leave it all behind, the only anchor point Vincenzo's hands on her, holding her still, and his tongue working his magic.

And when the end of the world finally came she called his name as the galaxies exploded and she was exploding too, a star blazing in the night, her soul flaming before dissolving into bliss.

Her hands were on him, stroking his shoulders absently as she lay back on the sofa, her face flushed, her mouth curving in a smile as old as time—that of a woman well satisfied.

He couldn't look away from her. He had her flavour in his mouth, a salty sweetness that had to be the most delicious thing he'd ever tasted, and he was desperate for more. Strange, when he'd never been desperate for a woman before. Needing sex, yes, but not a particular woman. Not like this.

Everything in him was urging him to pick her up and take her upstairs to his bed, because he had protection up there and he wanted to be inside her more than he wanted his next breath. Yet he didn't move, because he hadn't seen her smile, hadn't seen her face when she wasn't scared, and the sight of that smile made his chest get even tighter than it already was.

He'd done that to her. He'd been the one to give her that smile. And he couldn't remember the last time he'd made anyone feel good, made anyone feel happy. All he ever did was cause pain.

They deserve it though.

Yes, there was no question that they did. But…looking at Lucy's smile, he found he liked that he'd been the one to give her that. And he liked that he'd given her pleasure, made her call his name. Wiped the fear from her lovely hazel eyes…

This is not what you should be doing.

No, but he was going to do it anyway. He'd crossed the line of his own control, and anyway, to leave her now would be cruel and he couldn't do it. This would all be so new to her and he wanted to show her what more there was, what more that lovely body of hers was capable of.

Don't pretend you're not selfish. You want her for yourself too.

Oh, he wasn't pretending. He did want her for himself. And even though allowing himself to want a woman like her, a criminal, went against his own moral code, he wasn't going to let that stop him. He'd denied himself many things in pursuit of the justice he craved, but she wouldn't be one of them.

Her robe had fallen open, the red silk in perfect contrast to her pale skin, and her hair was spread everywhere, lush, dark lashes lying still on her cheeks. She was naked and everything he'd imagined. Full, perfect breasts with hard, berry-like nipples. Rounded hips and thighs, soft and graceful, with the pretty little nest of dark curls between.

He was hard now, so hard, and he couldn't wait any longer.

Vincenzo leaned forward and gathered her into his arms. Her eyelashes fluttered, her eyes opening as he straightened, holding her close.

'Where are we going?' Her head rested against his shoulder, her body utterly relaxed. She didn't sound concerned and her gaze was only curious.

'To my bedroom,' he said, unable to keep the roughness from his voice. 'We could go to yours, but there is no protection in your room.'

'Protection?' Her forehead creased. 'Oh… Oh, of course.' A shy little smile turned her vulnerable mouth. 'I was hoping that we might… That you would… I mean, I would like you to be my first.'

That soft confession shouldn't have affected him. It shouldn't have made his chest ache or cause bitterness to gather inside him, and yet it did both. An ache for the gesture of trust that it was, and bitterness because, God knew, he didn't deserve that trust.

He was going to hand her over to the police at

the end of this week and nothing would change his mind. He would be giving her to people who would put her in a cell and there would be no one to hold her if she panicked. No one to soothe her fear.

That thought shouldn't have been so bleak, shouldn't have made him feel so hollow inside. Shouldn't have made him so angry. But it was and it did. And he didn't understand it. If he'd had any sense at all, he would have put her down and walked away.

He wasn't going to, though. He was going to make love to her, because he wanted her. And he wasn't going to mention anything about the police or a cell or her guilt, because he wasn't going to scare her.

Tonight he didn't want her to be afraid of anything and, even though he had no idea why that would be important to him, he was going to accept it.

'There are better men for your first,' he said shortly.

'There might be,' she agreed. 'But I don't want them. I want you.'

Her honesty…it killed him. Made the knot of feelings inside him tighten unbearably, drawing attention as it did to his own failings and the gaps in his morality.

You're a hypocrite and you always have been.

Perhaps he was. After all, only a hypocrite would set himself on a course of justice, all the while knowing that he was a criminal himself. That the only reason he'd escaped paying for his own crimes was that he'd handed over his parents instead.

'You look so serious.' She leaned against him, looking up at him. 'What are you thinking about?'

But he wasn't going to talk about the past. That had no place here.

'You,' he said, and it wasn't far from the truth. 'Naked and in my bed.'

'Why? What is it about me that you want?'

He should tell her lies. Tell her that he had no idea why he wanted her, that she must have drugged him or bewitched him to make him so hard for her.

Yet he couldn't do that. He might be a liar and a hypocrite at heart, but he couldn't lie to her. Not about this. Not when she was small and soft in his arms, and the scent of apples and musk wove around him, making his groin ache. Making him want to put her down on the stairs right here, right now, and have her.

'You're beautiful,' he said, and again this was the truth. Her beauty was a secret thing, slowly revealing itself like a photo being developed, a gorgeous picture gradually coming into perfect focus. 'And you're very brave. And you're honest.'

'Beautiful? No, I don't think so. And I'm certainly not brave. I don't know if I—'

'Those things are all true,' he interrupted and not without gentleness, because she wasn't to argue with him on this. 'Whether you believe them or not.'

The look on her face softened and she reached up, her fingertips brushing his cheekbone in a touch that felt like fire against his skin. 'You're really very kind, aren't you?'

Kind. She thought he was kind.

He was nothing of the sort, but that was something else that he wasn't going to tell her. So he stayed silent instead as he came to his bedroom, kicking the door shut behind him as he went through the doorway. Then he carried her over to the big white bed and laid her down on it, before stepping back and stripping off his clothes.

She watched him, her glittering hazel eyes alive with curiosity and fascination and hunger, and when he was naked she reached for him in instinctive welcome.

That stole his breath, made his heart feel heavy in his chest. There was an affectionate, caring, and generous spirit beneath her wariness, and he was uncovering it, bit by bit.

You don't deserve it. You don't deserve her trust. You'll betray her like you betray everyone.

Vincenzo shoved that thought from his head as he reached for the protection in the bedside drawer. And locked it away as he prepared himself. Then he moved onto the bed with her, easing her onto her back and settling between her thighs. She made a small, throaty, satisfied sound as he did so, her body arching beneath his, pressing herself harder against him. Her hands were on his shoulders, stroking, as if she couldn't get enough of touching him.

'You're beautiful, too,' she murmured as he eased himself against the soft, damp heat between her thighs.

But he didn't want words now, not with her silky skin against his and the light, feminine musk of her scent intoxicating his senses, making the need hammer in his head so loudly that he could barely hear a thing. So he bent his head and took her lovely mouth, tasting the sweet fire that he was beginning to suspect lay at the heart of her. And she didn't protest, kissing him back, all shy inexperience and untutored hunger.

That sweetness felt unbearable to him all of a sudden, as did her inexperience. He didn't want any reminder of how vulnerable she was, or how alone and unprotected she'd been all her life. How she'd only ever been in the power of a man who'd hurt her. Scared her.

It made him feel things he didn't want to feel, emotions that he had no place for in his heart. He didn't want to protect her, care for her, keep her safe. All he wanted was to be inside her and this hunger for her sated.

He kissed her harder, with more demand, stroking down her body to the wetness that lay between her legs, his fingers circling the sensitive little bud. She gasped, trembling, her nails scraping over his skin. And that was better. That was much better than softness and vulnerability, better than the tightness in his chest and the ache in his heart.

So he kissed her harder still, deeper, nipping at her, biting at her until she moaned and her nails scratched him as she quivered and shifted restlessly beneath him. He was relentless, making her come against his hand, her breathing wild and ragged, and only then did he finally allow himself his own pleasure.

He wanted to thrust hard, show her that, though she might think him beautiful, he had no mercy to give her. That if she persisted in being soft with him, there would be nothing but pain in store for her. But he couldn't bring himself to do it. The thought of her pain in amongst this pleasure anathema to him.

So he pushed inside her slowly, carefully, watching her pretty face, searching for any signs of discomfort in the wide, dark eyes that looked up into his. She groaned, her gaze going even wider as he pushed deeper, but he saw no pain in it. Only a kind of wonder. As if he was a secret she'd always wanted to know, a secret that in the discovering was even better than she'd thought.

She was so hot. Slick. Perfect.

His brain blanked and for a moment he couldn't think of anything but her. Anything but the heat of her and the pleasure that was unfolding inside him, many-faceted and complex. Fascinating. Demanding.

He pushed his hands beneath her hips, tilting her, enabling him to go deeper, and she cried out, her hold on his shoulders almost painful. But she wasn't hurting, he could see that. She was as much in the grip of this pleasure as he was.

'Oh, Vincenzo,' she gasped, shuddering. 'Please, oh, please...'

And he moved, harder, deeper, his hands gripping her hips, losing himself in the tide of pleasure that washed over him, sweeping away the tightness in his chest and the poison in the centre of his soul. The corruption he could never escape, since it was part of him and would always be.

Sweeping away everything but the feel of her around him, the tight grip of her sex as she stiffened and arched beneath him, calling his name.

Everything but the pleasure that raced up his

spine and exploded in his head, an excoriating fire that gave him finally what he hadn't realised he'd been searching his whole life for: a single moment of purity.

It wouldn't last, though, and deep down he knew it. Which was why this could never happen again.

CHAPTER SEVEN

LUCY WOKE THE next morning knowing exactly where she was: Vincenzo's bedroom.

Sunshine came through a gap in the heavy white curtains, leaving a trail across the crisp white sheets, making it abundantly clear that she was alone.

A thread of disappointment wound through the pleasant, lazy, sated feeling inside her. She wanted him next to her so she could explore that powerful, masculine body in the daylight, discover what made his breath catch and turned his black eyes to flame.

She shivered deliciously as memories of the night before flooded through her. Of the feeling of him sliding inside her, pushing in deep, and how strange it had felt and how wonderful too. There hadn't been any pain, only a momentary discomfort that had gone almost as soon as she'd felt it. And then there had only been the most incredible feeling of connection, of being so close to another person. She'd never experienced anything like it.

His face had been stripped of everything but hunger, a fierce need that had echoed in her own soul. And for a brief, crystal-clear moment before the pleasure had washed it all away she'd seen something vulnerable in him. Something lost.

But the moment had been so brief that now, in the sunshine of the morning, she wondered if she'd seen it at all. Because what would make a man as strong and powerful as Vincenzo de Santi vulnerable? What would make him lost?

Curiosity tugged at her, that fatal flaw, but this time she indulged it. Staring at the ceiling, she remembered the research she'd conducted into him as she'd planned where to run to. The de Santi family was an old one, going back to medieval times when they'd been spies for a now lost Italian duchy, before an ancestor had found that there were more riches to be had in illegal activities.

In modern times they'd managed to stay one step ahead of the law, concerning themselves only with the jostling for precedence and constant need to earn respect among the crime families of Europe, fighting petty private wars and constantly stoking ancient feuds, and they probably would have continued in that vein if not for Vincenzo.

He'd betrayed his ancient heritage, his lineage, and reported his parents to the police in exchange for immunity.

Then he'd turned himself into the scourge of Europe, feared and loathed by the all the families who'd once considered the de Santis allies.

Lucy frowned at the ornate plastered ceiling.

What had made him turn his back on his family? Loyalty was the lifeblood of the old families, it was ingrained deep in their bones, but something had happened to Vincenzo. Something had shattered that loyalty. Or perhaps he'd never had it at all.

But no, that couldn't be. A man who held to such a difficult purpose as the one he'd chosen for himself wouldn't be a man with no loyalties or beliefs. If anything it was the opposite. But then, where did those loyalties lie? And to what? To justice? To making up for the sins of his family? Or was it something else?

What does it matter? In a week you'll be in custody and then you'll never see him again.

That thought hurt and so she ignored it in favour of slipping out of bed and heading for the shower in the en-suite bathroom. She washed herself, enjoying the cool water falling on various aching parts of her body, and when she was done she wrapped the familiar red robe around herself—which was the only item of clothing to hand—and went back to her own room.

The clothes he'd bought for her that had arrived the day before had been put away by Martina, and so she had to pull open the drawers on the big oak dresser and hunt through them. They were all very expensive, in beautiful fabrics, and all her size, and she, who'd never been much of a clothes person, found herself smiling as she pulled out a light, gauzy dress made out of pale green silk.

It was pretty, and when she put it on she could see how the colour brought out the green in her eyes. Immediately, her first thought was about what Vincenzo would think if he saw her in it and whether he would like it.

Your mother would have liked it too.

Oh, she would. She'd loved dressing Lucy up and Lucy had loved it too, but after Kathy had died she'd lost all interest in her appearance. Faint glimmers of interest were returning, though.

Perhaps it was silly to want to look nice for a man, especially a man who was still her enemy in many ways, but she decided she didn't care if it was silly or not and kept the dress on. She attempted to do something with her mass of hair, but, since she wasn't sure what, having never paid much attention to styling it before, she left it loose. Besides, she was hungry and wanted some breakfast.

She went downstairs to the terrace, where all the main meals of the day were served, hoping to find Vincenzo already there. But he wasn't. The table was set and food was on it, but the place was empty.

The disappointment she'd felt on waking returned and she turned around to go back inside and search for him, only to stop.

Why was she going to find him? What did she think she'd say? They'd spent the night together, that was all. No promises had been made, nothing had been said.

He'd given her pleasure and it had been the most incredible experience of her life, but he was still who he was. That hadn't changed. Nothing had changed.

But perhaps you have.

A strange feeling pulsed through her, part certainty, part strength. As if last night he'd given her some of his, along with the pleasure.

Yes, she had changed. She felt…different. More sure. Less afraid. And maybe if she had the urge to find him, to tell him that she wanted him again, then she should do it. He'd told her to be honest, that it was precious, so why shouldn't she be honest with him?

Avoiding things and hiding was what she'd done in the past and that had kept her safe. But safety was beginning to look overrated to her now. He'd given her a night without fear, a night of pleasure and warmth, and she wanted more.

She only had a few days left of it, after all— if she couldn't change his mind, that was.

First, though, she would eat.

Fifteen minutes later, full of coffee, bacon and some delicious pastries, Lucy went to find Martina to ask where Vincenzo was. Through some emphatic gestures, she understood that he was in his office and wasn't to be disturbed.

That gave her a moment's pause. Did that apply to just her or did that mean he didn't want to be disturbed by anyone? She only needed five minutes. That was allowable, wasn't it? Deciding that it was, she made her way to his office.

It was at the other end of the villa and the door was closed, so Lucy gave it a discreet knock. When there was no reply she stood there a second, debating, but then, nothing ventured, nothing gained, so she opened it quietly and went in.

The room was large, with fabulous views out over another terrace, a formal garden below that led all the way to the edge of the cliff and then the sea. A big desk stood near a set of high, arched windows and behind it stood the tall, powerful figure of Vincenzo.

He faced the windows with his back to the door, talking on the phone in his beautiful Italian, his voice calm and casual-sounding. His usual tone.

He wasn't in a suit today, wearing a pair of well-worn jeans that sat low on his hips and a faded blue T-shirt. As casual as his voice. A man doing a bit of light work on the weekend.

Except there was nothing casual about the tension that gathered in his broad shoulders and back, and even standing where she was by the door she could sense it. Was something bad happening? Did it have to do with her father?

She slipped into the room and closed the door behind her, moving over to the desk and pausing in front of it. Obviously hearing her footstep, he swung around, his obsidian gaze catching hers, the ferocity in it driving all the air from her lungs.

Had that fierceness always been there? Had she simply not seen it? Or was this new?

No, it had always been there, the driving force of his will allied with the flame of purpose. A man who would stop at nothing to get what he wanted or to do what was right. Who wouldn't let anything get in his way, not mercy, not sympathy, not tenderness. No soft feeling at all.

Yet…last night he'd been nothing but gentle with her—at least initially. Until she'd shown him that she didn't need gentleness.

He kept talking, the tone of his voice not changing one iota, holding her gaze with his. She couldn't breathe, couldn't move. The seething tension that gathered around him held her fast.

Something was wrong. He was angry. No, more than that. He was furious.

Male anger was always something to be wary of. Her father's rages had been terrifying and she'd seen the consequences of that rage first-hand. After her mother had died, being in his vicinity had always made her go icy with fear and she tried to avoid him at all costs when he was like that.

Yet, even though Vincenzo seemed no less angry, she wasn't scared. His was a coldly controlled anger and the threat of violence that hovered around him wasn't directed at her. He told her he would never hurt her and she'd believed him then; she believed him now too.

She didn't back away and leave the room the way she might have done even a week earlier. Instead she lifted her chin and stood there, waiting for him to finish. She'd been going to ask him why he'd left her that morning, but now she wanted to know why he was so angry. Was it her father? Business? What?

Quite suddenly he disconnected the call and flung the phone back down on the desk with a clatter. 'What do you want?' There was an edge to his cool voice. 'I told Martina I wasn't to be disturbed.'

Lucy took a breath, studying the hard cast of his features and the black glitter of his eyes. 'Why are you angry?'

'Why do you think? I gave orders that I wasn't to be interrupted and yet here you are.'

'That's not why.' Something more was going on here, she was sure of it. The hot breath of his fury was too intense to be about a mere interruption. 'Is it my father?'

He muttered something vicious under his breath and looked away, the tension pouring off him.

The urge to go around the desk and put her hands on those hard, muscled shoulders to ease him was almost overwhelming. But they'd only had one night together and she couldn't presume anything. He probably wouldn't welcome it anyway.

She clasped her hands in front of her instead. 'Vincenzo?'

'You should leave.' The words were bitten out. 'I'm not in the mood for conversation.'

'Why? What's happened?'

He lifted his head, his gaze clashing with hers again. The darkness in it made it hard to breathe. 'You happened, *civetta.*'

Shock slid down her spine. She stared at him, not understanding. 'What do you mean, I happened?'

He straightened, a muscle in his jaw leaping. 'Last night you compromised my moral code and it cannot happen again.' The anger threading through his voice was like hot metal piercing a block of ice, making his accent more pronounced. 'I do not sleep with my prisoners.'

Oh. So that was the issue. *She* was the issue. And he regretted it.

A heavy disappointment settled in her stomach, though she knew she had no right to be disappointed. There had been no promises made, no indication that it would happen again. She'd just assumed, because it had been so good...

For you. But perhaps not for him.

Her mouth dried, the disappointment turning inward, growing sharp edges. 'I...see,' she said huskily. 'I didn't mean—'

'You didn't mean to sleep with me? Is that what you're trying to say? You didn't mean to compromise me? Or cause me to forget everything I stand for?' He gave a harsh laugh. 'You overestimate your charms, Miss Armstrong. It wasn't you and your lovely body, believe me. It was my own weakness.'

The edges were razor-sharp, cutting her, pain seeping through her. She wanted to turn away and leave the room, run away and hide. She'd thought that what had happened between them had been special, had been precious, and now he was looking at her as if it had meant nothing. As if she'd meant nothing.

He'd told her that she was worth savouring, but…had he not meant it?

Are you worth it, though? After what your mother sacrificed for you? You were where you shouldn't have been and that's all your fault.

The thought ran like acid through her. No, she wasn't going to think about that. Yet she couldn't pretend to herself that his opinion didn't matter to her, either. Pretending wouldn't change the emotion sitting in her heart. It did matter, because the night with him *had* been special and it *had* meant something. And maybe she was assuming that because it had been that way for her, it had been that way for him, too. But clearly she was wrong. While she'd felt changed on some fundamental level, he simply felt angry.

That hurt, she couldn't deny it. She didn't expect anything from him—an emotional attachment was the last thing she wanted—but she wasn't going to act as if it meant nothing either.

He'd told her to be honest and so she would, both with herself and with him, and if he didn't like that then too bad.

'Yet it's me you're apparently angry with.' She pushed her glasses up her nose. 'Shouldn't you be yelling at yourself in that case?'

He gave a short laugh that held no amusement. 'I should, yes.'

'You might regret what happened last night, Vincenzo, but I don't.' She lifted her chin, holding his ferocious gaze. 'I don't regret any second of it. In fact, that's why I came to find you. I wanted to know why you left and whether you wanted to—'

'No,' he cut her off harshly. 'I will not sleep with you again.'

But she didn't let his tone get to her. 'I wasn't going to ask if you would, only if you wanted to.'

The tension gathered tighter around him, like

a fist closing, and all of a sudden it was clear to her what that tension was and where his anger was coming from: he *did* want to. He wanted to badly, because she knew that fierce look in his eyes. She'd seen it the night before as he'd moved inside her. It was hunger, fierce desire, and denial.

He was at war with himself and what he wanted.

The raw feeling inside her eased; she'd been hoping he might feel the same way she had about the night before, but she hadn't been sure. Now it seemed clear that, despite himself, it had been good for him. And that he wanted more.

Except she didn't know what to do, whether to let him put her at a distance or to close it.

'I do not want to,' he bit out, his whole posture rigid with tension.

'You told me honesty was precious,' she said quietly. 'And yet you're lying.'

There were black flames in his eyes, his temper a cold fire. 'Don't presume to know me, *civetta*. You have no idea—'

'You want me, Vincenzo. I can see it in your eyes.'

The muscle in the side of his jaw leapt again.

'It won't happen, Lucy. I've already told you that.'

'Then why are you still so angry?' She came closer, the width of his desk all that separated them. 'If it's not going to happen again, then why should what's already happened matter?'

He said nothing, staring at her, the panther starving for his prey.

She swallowed, the sound of her heartbeat getting louder in her head.

Perhaps she should leave after all. Perhaps it was selfish of her to force this issue with him. He was a man of strict principles and she was essentially asking him to go against everything he believed in. Then again, he was also a man of strong passions, passions that he hadn't given in to and yet clearly needed release from.

Would it be wrong to encourage him to release them with her? He'd already done so the night before after all, and a second time couldn't hurt. And anyway, when was the last time anyone had made him feel good? Did he even have anyone?

Lucy put her fingertips on the desk, steadying herself. 'Do you want to know why I'm here, Vincenzo?'

'No.'

She ignored him. 'I came to tell you that last night was special to me. That you made me feel…so very good. And so very safe. I've been afraid for so long, but I wasn't last night. I wasn't afraid at all, not for one second. And I…want that again.'

The flames in his eyes burned like cold wildfire. 'You are my prisoner.'

'So you keep saying. And I know you care about that, but I don't.'

'You should care. I'm going to hand you over to the police and they're going to put you in a cell, and there will be no one to ease your fear then, *civetta*. No one to hold you or calm you.'

Something vulnerable inside her shivered, but she ignored it.

You won't be able to change his mind. He'll never release you.

She ignored that too.

'I know that,' she said and didn't look away.

'You will get no gentleness from me. No mercy.'

Lucy arched a brow, her own temper stirring. 'Did I ask for any?'

He muttered something low and vicious in

Italian, then continued in English, 'You don't know what you're asking for.'

She lifted her chin even higher. 'Then show me.'

There was only the desk between them. Only a paltry length of wood that he could have reached across and dragged her over the top of at any time. It was all he could do to stop himself from doing just that.

She looked so beautiful this morning in a green silk dress that made her skin look creamy and deepened the chestnut of her hair, making her eyes seem greener too. The fabric was sheer and he could see the curvaceous shape of her through it, and it made him so hard he could barely think.

Then again, he'd been trying to think all morning and been unable to, his mind full of her. He'd thought going to his study and burying himself in work would be the answer, but it wasn't. Even the news he'd just received, about how Armstrong wanted to do a deal for her return, hadn't distracted him.

The whole night had been a mistake and he knew it. That moment of clarity, of purity, when pleasure had annihilated all thought and he'd lost himself in the darkness of her eyes, had been the turning point. If it had only been sex between them, if she'd been just another in the long line of women he'd had before, then it wouldn't have mattered. He'd have taken his pleasure as often as he could with her and the rest of the world be damned.

But she wasn't just another woman and it wasn't only sex. He'd known it wouldn't be the moment she'd told him that she wanted him to be her first. And it certainly hadn't felt like only sex when he'd touched her, when he'd buried himself inside her.

There was something in the way she looked at him, the way she touched him, as if he was her white knight, a man who would save her, not lock her in a cell. A man who would protect her, keep her safe. A man she trusted...

But he could never be those things for her. Not if he didn't want to compromise his entire life up to this point. Justice had always been his driving force and he didn't allow himself to be swayed or manipulated. Wouldn't allow his emotions to be twisted or turned the way his mother had twisted and turned them. Yet somehow Lucy had done both.

Correction. She hadn't done it; he'd allowed it to happen. The problem was him, not her. He'd been weak. He should be burning with the holy fire of justice, not the sensual flame of desire.

Yet that flame wouldn't go out and now she was here, so close, offering him more of what his body so desperately wanted, and the need inside him wouldn't be leashed.

She was a criminal, though. She'd broken the law. She was his prisoner. She was everything he'd been fighting against and he couldn't allow himself to have her.

But why not? She wants you. And no one need know. You've told her that you won't be kind and you won't show mercy, and that you're still going to hand her over to the law, so she will have no expectations. After all, you've already crossed the line once...

His hands clenched tight, all the reasons for holding back suddenly seeming spurious. Maybe he was turning this into a bigger issue than it needed to be. Yes, he'd thought the night before had been about more than sex, but it didn't need to continue like that. She wasn't a virgin any more. And besides, it would only be for another few days and then the time limit he'd imposed would be up. He would give her over to the police and hopefully by then this madness—because it couldn't be anything other than madness—would have left him.

The look in her eyes from across the desk now was all challenge, an emerald glow glittering in the depths. A familiar emerald glow. It had burned bright as she'd climaxed beneath him, his name torn from her all husky and raw.

Show me, she'd said, and so maybe he would. Maybe she needed to see what kind of man he was at heart.

He unclenched his hands and moved around the side of his desk, approaching her slowly. She didn't move, watching him come closer, her gaze steady. There was nothing wary or guarded about it now—she was an open book, her desire for him easily readable in her pretty face.

The urge to take that face between his palms and kiss her, give her more gentleness, was strong, but he resisted it. He'd told her he had no mercy and so he would give her none. And if she wanted to know what that was like, then he *would* show her.

'On your knees,' he ordered coldly.

She blinked, but after a moment's hesitation she knelt on the silk rug in front of him, her head tilting back as she looked up at him. Pink tinged her cheekbones, her eyes a deep, fascinating green behind the lenses of her glasses.

His breath caught, the ache in his groin almost overwhelming now. He reached down and took her glasses off, laying them carefully on the desk beside them.

'What do you want me to do?' she asked breathlessly.

There was no fear either in her voice or her expression, only a sensual curiosity that made his pulse accelerate. There were so many things he could teach her, that they would both enjoy, and why not? Why not take the entire day? If he was going to do this, he might as well commit himself whole-heartedly.

'I'll tell you.' He dropped his hands to the fastenings of his jeans and undid the button, drawing down the zip. Her gaze followed his movements, the pink in her cheeks deepening into red.

'Give me your hand,' he murmured.

She did so without hesitation and he took it in his, guiding her fingers to him, showing her how to draw him out of his boxers and jeans, then how to hold him in her fist. Her touch was searing and it was all he could do to make himself go slowly. Because even though he had no mercy, she was still new to this and he still couldn't bring himself to frighten her.

'Now,' he went on, his voice husky as the pressure of her fist around him sent pure electricity to every nerve-ending he had. 'Take me in your mouth.'

She obeyed, taking him in as if she'd been waiting her whole life to taste him, and the second the heat of her mouth encircled him he had to grit his teeth against the urge to thrust deep.

Instead, he dropped both hands to her hair and threaded his fingers through it, guiding her mouth on him gently and showing her what to do. Encouraging her with whispered commands to use her teeth and her tongue, when to suck and when to release, teaching her the rhythm he preferred.

She was eager and didn't balk at anything he asked of her, the softness of her lips and her inexperienced enthusiasm somehow making it ten thousand times more erotic than what he'd had from other women.

He watched her face, pleasure sweeping through him, making his heart race and the blood pump hard in his veins. The feeling of that vulnerable mouth on him was exquisite, something he'd never forget, and when she closed her eyes as if he was the most delicious thing she'd ever tasted, and made a soft, husky sound in the back of her throat, he knew he wasn't going to last.

His fingers tightened in her hair, pulling her head away from him, and as he did so her eyes opened. 'Oh,' she breathed. 'Did I do something wrong?'

But he was beyond speech.

He pulled her to her feet lifted her onto the desk and set her on top of it. Then he pulled up the hem of her dress, gathering all the green silk up to her waist, before pushing her thighs apart. He spent a breathless minute finding some protection in his wallet, ripping open the packet and rolling down the latex. Then he pulled her to the edge of the desktop and dipped a hand between her legs.

Her eyes were very wide, the hazel gone smoky and dark with desire. And as his fingers touched her slick flesh she shuddered, gasping softly.

She was soft and hot, and very wet, and when he positioned himself, pushing slowly inside her, she welcomed him with a sigh of satisfaction. 'Yes,' she murmured. 'Oh, Vincenzo... yes...'

And he felt that peace again. That stillness. As if he'd been in a room full of unwelcome noise and someone had shut the door, leaving him with blissful quiet.

Nothing but heat. Nothing but pleasure. Nothing but peace.

Her thighs closed around his waist, holding him tight inside her, and then her hands were in his hair, pulling his mouth down on hers, kissing him so sweetly, making him feel as if all of this was new to him too, new and wondrous.

The war inside him ceased and he let himself have this moment of ease, beginning to move, allowing the pleasure to set its own pace, slow and languorous.

She sighed and arched against him, and he paused once to pull her dress off over her head and get rid of her bra, getting rid of his T-shirt too, so that there was nothing between them, nothing but her silky, damp skin against his. And then he kept moving, the thrust of his hips driving them both closer and closer to the edge.

Her kisses became hungry and he gave her back the same hunger, gripping her hips so he could move harder and deeper, the easy pace becoming something more desperate. She tore her mouth from his, kissing his neck and his shoulders, her tongue tasting the hollow of his throat as if she couldn't get enough of him, frantic, feverish words spilling out of her.

He'd forgotten he was supposed to have no mercy and that he wasn't going to give her gentleness. Stroking her back and soothing her were automatic and instinctive, as was the need to ease her desperation. He took her hand and guided it down where they were joined, putting his fingers over hers and showing her what to do to increase her pleasure. She writhed as he did so, her body desperate for release, giving harsh little pants and moaning against his neck, so he pressed her finger hard against the bundle of nerves where she was most sensitive, allowing her to tumble over the edge.

And only when she convulsed around him, did he allow himself to thrust hard and deep and fast, letting himself fall over that edge too, tumbling end over end, and down into peace with her.

CHAPTER EIGHT

LUCY TRIED TO crawl out from under the blanket thrown over one of the sofas in the salon downstairs, only for a powerful male arm to hook around her waist and draw her back in again.

'No, you don't,' Vincenzo growled, pulling her up against his very hot and very naked body. 'I haven't finished with you yet.'

She gave a long-suffering sigh, running a hand down the warm, velvety skin of his back, loving the feel of all that hard muscle beneath her palm, despite the fact that she'd spent most of the day running her hands all over his body. 'But I'm hungry. Lunch was hours ago.'

He moved, settling himself over her, his weight a delicious pressure pinning her down. 'You're always hungry.'

'So are you.' She shivered as he pressed his mouth to her throat.

'It's true.' He moved lower, nuzzling against

her breast. 'Luckily I have all the food I need right here.'

'Yes, but I don't.' The word ended on a gasp as he took her nipple in his mouth, the hot pressure making everything inside her go tight.

She couldn't want him again, surely? They'd done nothing else all day.

After the encounter in his office that morning, he'd been insatiable, taking her upstairs almost immediately and laying her out across the bed, setting about exploring every inch of her body. He'd been slow and relentless and she was pretty sure she'd screamed. More than once.

He'd sent Martina away for the rest of the day after that and forbidden his security to come into the house. Then he'd made her lunch himself, feeding it to her as she lay in bed wrapped only in a sheet. Once lunch had finished, he'd taken her yet again, and she'd fallen asleep in his arms. She'd woken to find herself downstairs on the sofa in the salon, the doors open, and a naked Vincenzo sitting on the floor leaning back against the sofa, doing something on his laptop. He'd known she was awake instantly and had put aside the computer, joining her on the cushions. They'd lost another hour like that and now she was feeling well rested, physically sated, and ravenous.

In other words, she'd never felt better in her entire life. Apart from being hungry, of course.

She pushed at his muscular shoulders. 'Vincenzo. Food.'

Finally, he lifted his head and gave her a measuring look. 'Very well. But you let me organise it, yes?'

'Okay.' She had no problems with that. If he wanted to feed her the way he'd fed her lunch, she was more than happy.

But Vincenzo clearly had a bigger plan than a simple meal in mind, because he made her stay where she was for at least half an hour, before finally coming to get her and leading her down a couple of hallways and out to a small private terrace shielded from view by trees and potted bushes.

A big outdoor bath sat on the stone floor of the terrace and steam rose from the water. Candlelight leapt and flickered from holders placed on various surfaces, casting a gentle glow over everything.

Her chest constricted as he urged her towards the bath, his hand gentle at her back.

'This is beautiful, Vincenzo,' she said huskily. 'Is it for me?'

'Yes.' He eased the robe he'd put around her off her shoulders. 'There's no beach here and it's too late to swim from the rocks. We have a pool built into the cliff but it's a bit cool at night. I thought you'd enjoy being outside and in some warm water in case you're sore.'

She was slightly...achy. And parts of her that were a little chafed would like some warm water to ease them. She definitely would enjoy that.

Then again, she already was enjoying everything he'd already given her, just as she was very determinedly only thinking about what was happening now and not what would happen in a few days, when he handed her over. It wasn't relevant to this moment and, since this moment was all she had, she'd enjoy every single second of it.

She slipped naked into the bath, the water delightfully scented and warm.

'I'll be back,' Vincenzo murmured and disappeared into the house.

Sighing, Lucy leaned her head back on the bath, loving the soothing effect of the water and the sound of the waves at the base of the cliffs below the house. The stars studded the black sky, the candlelight flickering, and yet another moment presented itself. A moment of peace and tranquillity and utter safety.

Her father couldn't reach her here. No one could. She was protected by Vincenzo and he'd let nothing touch her.

He will give you up, you know this…

But that thought wasn't part of the moment and so she ignored it, counting the stars above her head and letting herself drift in the water.

She must have drifted to sleep too, because she opened her eyes maybe only seconds later, to find Vincenzo had returned and had set a tray of food plus a bottle of white wine and wine glasses down on a stone table near the bath. He'd pulled on a pair of jeans, but wore nothing else, and so she lay there for a few moments, watching the play of muscles moving beneath his tanned skin as he opened the wine and poured it.

And she didn't need to see clearly to know he was beautiful. Stunningly masculine and so physically powerful. Also so fierce and passionate, and not at all the cold, judgmental angel he'd appeared to be when she'd first met him.

He'd told her that he had no mercy and yet with her he'd been nothing but kind. Demanding, true, yet also gentle. And his ruthlessness hid a protective nature that she found almost unbearably attractive.

You feel something for him...

Lucy forced her gaze away, the water around her suddenly not quite as warm as it had been. She was only admiring him. It didn't mean anything emotionally.

Her skin prickled and she looked up again to find that he'd turned from the table and was now watching her, a familiar expression of hunger on his blunt, aristocratic features. 'I was going to ask if you wanted some dinner now, but maybe we could wait five minutes. I suddenly have a very strong urge to have a bath.'

She flushed at the heat in his eyes. 'Dinner first,' she said firmly. 'It would be very unfortunate if I starved to death at a vital moment.'

He stared at her a second and then, much to her delight, his hard mouth curved into one of the most glorious smiles she'd ever seen. It softened the stern lines of his face, making him seem much more approachable and incredibly sexy. 'That would, indeed, be unfortunate. Perhaps I'll wait, then.' He picked up a large white towel he'd draped over a nearby stone bench. 'Come, *civetta*. Get out of the bath and let me dry you.'

She could have done it herself, but she didn't want to, getting out of the bath and letting him dry her off and wrap her in the lovely red silk robe. It made her feel cared for, and it had been a long time since she'd felt cared for, so she would let herself enjoy it while it lasted.

Not that you deserve it. Not when your mother died because of you.

Lucy ignored the thought.

A few minutes later she was seated on one of the stone benches, cushioned by mounds of pillows, a plate full of cold meats, salad, cheeses and delicious fresh-baked bread in her lap. A glass of wine sat on the back of the bench at her elbow, while Vincenzo lounged in a chair opposite, ostensibly making sure her plate was full. To 'build up her strength' since it was apparent he had plans for the rest of the evening. Plans that obviously featured her.

'This is wonderful,' she said, picking up an olive. 'Thank you.'

He inclined his head in wordless acknowledgement, sipping on his wine as she slowly chewed the olive, relishing the sharp, salty taste.

'This whole place is wonderful,' she went on, gesturing around them at the villa and its grounds. 'Did you come here a lot as a child?'

'Not often. I do spend a lot of time here now, however.'

'Oh? Why is that?'

'The *palazzo* is…medieval and dark. I prefer this villa. It's much lighter, and being near the sea is pleasant.'

There was something in his voice she couldn't place. An edge. She wanted to ask him what it meant, but the mood between them was relaxed and easy and she didn't want to upset it.

'I think that was the worst thing about the house in Cornwall,' she said instead. 'It was near the sea, but it had no view. I could hear the waves but I could never see them.'

'You weren't allowed to go out at all?' This

time there was no edge in his voice, the question utterly neutral. 'Not even for a drive?'

'No.' She didn't see the harm in telling him. It was only the truth, after all. 'Perhaps I could have argued for a trip to the beach, but I couldn't see the point. It would only make me want what I couldn't have.' The story of her life, really. 'Easier to take a virtual trip via my computer.'

Vincenzo frowned. 'So you never left the house?'

'Dad would sometimes take me to London.' She reached for her wine and took a sip herself, enjoying the cool bite of it. 'But not often. I didn't like going anyway. It meant meetings with some of his contacts and friends and they scared me.'

Vincenzo's frown became fierce, the glitter of his eyes sharper. 'Why? Did they hurt you?'

She could hear the promise of retribution in his voice and it set up a small, warm glow inside her, even though she knew it shouldn't. 'No. Dad wouldn't have been pleased with them if they had and they were afraid of him.'

'You were afraid of him too.'

'I was,' she agreed. 'I am.'

'And yet you escaped him.' Vincenzo tilted his head, his black gaze focusing on her as if he'd never seen anything so interesting in his life. 'What made you run, *civetta*? Was it opportunity or had you been planning it?'

They hadn't talked of anything personal the whole day and she'd been more than happy with that. But now tension crawled through her. Talking about this would involve explaining about the promise she'd made to her mother, and how her mother had died, and the reason for it...

Then he'll know exactly how guilty you really are.

A kernel of ice settled in the pit of her stomach. She didn't want to tell him. She wanted him to keep thinking of her as someone worth savouring, someone worth taking care of. She didn't want this warmth between them to end. There was still a chance she could convince him to change his mind about handing her over to the police, but if she told him the real reason for her mother's death, that chance would be gone.

She looked down at her plate, picking up a red cherry tomato and eating that to give herself a moment or two to think, even though her appetite had vanished.

No, she couldn't lie to him. He valued her honesty, which meant she'd have to tell him the truth, face his judgment. Accept her own guilt, because she couldn't hide from it any longer.

Lucy gathered her courage and met his gaze head-on. 'I ran because of a promise I made to my mother. She wanted me to survive, get free any way I could, but it took me a long time to be brave enough to do it. I killed her, you see. The story was that she tripped and fell against a window, sliced her arm, and bled to death. But that's not what happened.' Her jaw ached, but she forced herself to go on. 'Dad had a lot of secret meetings and I was curious about them. I'd always try and eavesdrop, pretend I was a spy, stupid things like that. I knew I wasn't supposed to. Mum warned me not to, that Dad would get very angry if he caught me, and there would be consequences. But… I couldn't help myself.'

She took a breath, her hands now in her lap, her fingers twisting. 'He did catch me that day. And Mum was right, he was furious. He was going to hit me, but she put herself between him and me, and caught the blow instead. It knocked her into a window, which broke, cutting a major artery.' She felt very cold all of a sudden, as if she'd been plunged head first into a pool of snow melt. 'Dad did nothing. He just walked out, leaving me to try and help her. There was so much blood…and I couldn't.' Lucy's throat closed up. 'She made me promise to escape, to have a life away from him. To be happy. And then…she died.'

There was no expression at all on Vincenzo's face, but a fierce light burned in his midnight eyes. 'Lucy,' he said softly.

'And you're right,' she went on, because she had to say it now. 'I am a criminal. I'm guilty of all those crimes I committed for my dad. But mainly I'm guilty of being the reason for her death. If I'd only listened to her, if I hadn't been so curious, so s-stupid, if I'd just done what I was told, Dad wouldn't have found me. He wouldn't have got so angry. And he wouldn't have tried to hit me, and then Mum wouldn't have died. I killed her, Vincenzo. It was my fault.'

Of course it is. And you deserve everything that's coming to you.

Fear came bubbling up at the insidious voice inside her head, a black wave of it, and she had to turn away, unable to face Vincenzo's dark gaze and the judgment that would no doubt be there, sticking like a splinter in her heart.

She didn't know when his opinion of her had begun to matter so much, but it did, and she couldn't bear it. She didn't want the way he looked at her or treated her, with so much gentleness and kindness, to change, yet it would, and she couldn't avoid that.

She deserved his condemnation, not soft candles, and delicious food, and a warm bath.

Face it like your mother faced her death, coward.

Lucy swallowed and lifted her head, determined now, forcing herself to look into his eyes. Because her mother hadn't hesitated to put herself in physical danger to protect her, and so she couldn't hesitate now.

'I appreciate everything you've done for me, Vincenzo,' she said, her voice hoarse. 'But I don't deserve it. Not any of it.'

She'd prepared herself to meet his judgment—that much was clear from the look on her face.

And, given how pale she'd gone, it was obvious that she was expecting that judgment not to be in her favour.

He hadn't meant to have this discussion with her, not here, not now. But that was his own fault. He'd been the one to ask her why she'd escaped when she had. And, of course, she'd answered him with her customary honesty.

And he wasn't sure what horrified him more: that she blamed herself for her mother's death or that she expected him to blame her as well.

You told her she was guilty, that she was a criminal.

That was true, he had. But how could he think she was either? After that?

Her little chin was lifted, her eyes shadowed behind the lenses of her glasses, the green lost in the darkness. She was brave to tell him what she had. And it had cost her. He could see the cost in the gleam of tears she was trying not to let fall, that fogged her glasses, and in the tension that surrounded her.

She'd sat up so straight on the stone bench, telling him in a steady voice about her mother's death. About how her mother had defended her, protected her, and in the end bled to death right in front of her. And for that, Lucy blamed herself.

'I don't deserve it. Not any of it...'

She was a criminal and she was guilty. The crimes she'd committed for her father couldn't be erased. But what she wasn't guilty of was her mother's death.

'How old were you when that happened?' he asked carefully.

'Seven.'

Dear God. She'd watched her mother die at seven…

His heart contracted painfully tight. He wanted to put his wine down, cross the space between them, gather her into his arms, take the pain he saw in her eyes away with his touch. But he had to make this clear to her first.

The law was a logical thing and emotion had no part in justice. And he wanted her to know, unequivocally, that, from a legal standpoint at least, she was blameless.

'And did you stab your mother with that piece of glass?' he asked.

She blinked. 'No. She fell against the window because Dad hit her.'

'She died of blood loss, yes?'

Lucy nodded and he could see her swallow. This was so very painful for her. Her jaw and shoulders were so tight. She looked very fragile, so very vulnerable.

His heart contracted even tighter, but he ignored it.

'You could not have killed your mother, Lucy,' he said in a neutral voice. 'If you had picked up a piece of glass and stabbed her with it, then that would be a different story. But you didn't.'

She shook her head. 'I didn't listen. I should have—'

'You were seven,' he cut across her gently. 'You were a child. What seven-year-old listens to everything their parents tell them?'

The look on her face was bleak. 'She was afraid and yet she still protected me. She stepped in front of Dad and took the blow meant for me. And if she hadn't she wouldn't have fallen against the glass and—' Her voice cracked.

Vincenzo put his glass down then and rose from his chair, giving in to his own instinct, because the sight of those barely suppressed tears… He couldn't sit there, letting her cry, and not offer any comfort. He couldn't.

Crossing to the bench she was on, he sat down and pulled her into his arms before she could protest, holding her the way he had days ago in his office in London.

Immediately she turned her head, burying her face against his chest, her shoulders shaking in a silent sob, and it made him ache that her instinct was to turn to him for comfort. It made him want to hold her tight, protect her, be deserving of the trust she'd put in him.

He disentangled her momentarily to take her glasses off so they didn't hurt her, laying them down on the arm of the bench next to him, then he gathered her in his arms once more and held her close, stroking her thick, glossy curls.

'She was only doing what any mother would,' he said. 'She was protecting her child.' His own mother, for all her faults, would have done the same. But not out of any maternal instinct. She would have done it for her own ends, not his.

'Sometimes I don't understand why.' Lucy's voice was muffled. 'Sometimes all I can think is why? Why did she protect me? What was it about me that was worth dying for? And if she hadn't protected me, then she wouldn't have died and maybe other people might not have got hurt. My father might not have used me—'

'You cannot think like that, *civetta*,' he interrupted quietly. 'The past is something you can't change, so there is no point in going over all the what-ifs and might-have-beens. You did not kill your mother. She made a choice to protect you and she made that choice because she loved you. If you are going to assign blame to anyone, assign it to your father. He is the villain here, not you.'

'A villain I worked for. I did everything he told me to and if I hadn't been so afraid...'

Vincenzo tightened his fingers in her hair, drawing her head back. Her face was wet with tears, her eyes red-rimmed and her nose pink. She looked so sad and yet so unutterably lovely. How had he ever thought her plain?

'You cannot blame yourself for that, Lucy.' He put force into the words. 'You escaped him. You were afraid, but you made a promise to your mother and so you didn't let that stop you. In the end, you were brave and you escaped, and that's the only thing that matters.'

But pain lingered in her eyes. 'If I had truly

been brave, I would have stood up to him. My mother did. She knew he would hurt her and yet she stood up to him anyway. I should have done that. Should have refused to do all those things, gone to the police.' A tear ran down her cheek. 'And I didn't. I...allowed him to keep me prisoner because I was just terrified.'

He cupped her cheek in his palm, his thumb brushing away the tear. 'You had reason to be terrified, *civetta*. He is ruthless and violent and he would have hurt you very badly if you'd done any of those things.'

Even the thought of what Armstrong could have done to her made Vincenzo's blood run cold and a red haze of rage descend over his vision.

Does she really matter that much to you?

But he ignored that thought entirely.

Lucy shook her head. 'Mum was afraid of him, but she didn't let it stop her. She was so brave, while I just sat in my room cowering for years. She would have been so ashamed.'

'No,' he said flatly and with absolute conviction, tightening his fingers in her hair for emphasis. 'To see you now, she would have been proud. And she would have thought her death worthwhile if it kept you from harm.'

Lucy's lovely face was tearstained, and she looked at him, as if she was searching for something that only he could give her. 'How do you know that?'

He didn't, of course. He didn't know anything about loving mothers who protected their children. But he did know this little *civetta* and what she'd done for him. Because she had changed him. With her honesty and her trust, with the heat of her passion and the cold grip of her fear. With the heart she wore on her sleeve…

'Because you are worth saving, Lucy Armstrong,' he said quietly.

Lucy flushed and the pain in her eyes eased, and he found himself going on, for what reason he didn't know. Maybe because he didn't want her to feel alone.

'And because I have done things I regret too, things I cannot change no matter how I wish I could.'

She blinked, tears glittering on the ends of her lashes. 'What things?'

He shouldn't tell her. No one knew. And he

hadn't thought he'd want anyone to know either. But somehow it felt wrong to hold this back, to let her know that she wasn't as alone in the world as she might think. That he understood in a way few other people would.

You weren't supposed to let your emotions become a part of this.

No, but it was too late for that now and he knew it. His emotions were engaged already. All he could do now was to make sure he didn't allow them to get in the way of what needed to be done.

'I never knew what my family was.' He kept his voice quiet, his thumb moving on her cheek. 'My mother maintained a fiction of the proud de Santi legacy, an aristocratic family of warriors fighting to protect what was theirs. I believed her. A proud de Santi prince, she called me, and that's what I believed myself to be. I was arrogant and spoiled. So sure of myself and my place in the world. I didn't see what was wrong with that place until it was too late. Until people died because of what I'd become.'

Lucy's eyes were very wide. 'What did you become?'

'I became complicit.' He couldn't stop the bitterness that coloured his tone. 'Though I was always complicit, I just chose not to see it.'

A deep crease lay etched between her brows. 'What did you choose not to see?'

Even now he didn't like to think about it. But he couldn't not tell her, not when she'd shared what had happened to her.

'My mother was beautiful and very loving, but she was also a de Santi through and through. I wasn't a son so much as her tool. She used me from a young age, mostly as a spy or a distraction, since children could be useful for manipulating adults and since they were so easy to manipulate themselves. She told me I was her brave soldier and that if I wanted to be a general, I had to prove my worth and follow orders.'

He could feel the creeping dread of the night he never thought about. The inexplicable dread that he always tried to hold at bay, because nothing had ever really happened. Or, at least, that was what he'd told himself. What he'd been telling himself for years…

'We were at the opera one night in Naples, and at the end of the production my mother pointed to a woman in the theatre foyer and told me to bring her to the alleyway a couple of doors down from the theatre. She said that if I pretended to be lost, and cry a few tears, no one would question it. I was seven and I loved my mother with all my heart. I only wanted to make her happy, and so I did what she asked.' Years ago now, and yet that dread still wrapped around him and squeezed him tight. 'The woman was so kind. She hugged me when she found me crying, and gave me a sweet, and she followed me when I told her to come with me to the place I'd last seen my family. She held my hand and told me a funny story...' He stopped, took a breath, and then went on, 'There was a van in the alleyway. And when we approached, the door opened and some men got out. They grabbed her and pushed her into the van and drove off. She didn't even have a chance to scream.'

Lucy's gaze darkened. 'Oh, Vincenzo.'

He could hear the sympathy in her voice, but he knew he didn't deserve any of it. 'My mother was so pleased with me. And I felt proud that I'd done what she wanted me to do. And yet... I couldn't stop seeing that woman's face as they grabbed her. The look of fear on it. Even then I knew that something had happened to her, but I didn't let myself remember it or think about it. But that memory was always there, and then Gabriella happened.'

Lucy placed a hand on his chest, her palm a small ember of heat. 'Gabriella?'

He didn't want to talk about this either, but it was too late for silence.

'When I was twelve, Mama encouraged me to be friends with the daughter of a rival family. She was my age and wasn't afraid of me like the other kids were. I liked that very much. I didn't question why my mother wanted me to be Gabriella's friend, I just let her encourage it because it suited me too.'

'Other kids were afraid of you?'

'Because of my family. The de Santis were very much feared, though I didn't understand why at the time.' He paused, the bitterness sinking deeper into his heart. 'I liked that though. I liked being the de Santi prince that everyone was afraid of. And I was very loyal to my mother, wouldn't hear a bad word said about her. I ignored the rumours and doubts that I picked up as I grew older. That the de Santis were a family of murderers and traitors, and that my mother was the most feared of all, because of her reputation for brutality. I didn't believe them. Mama was small and beautiful and adored me. I couldn't even conceive of her being brutal.' Tension wound through him, though he tried not to let it. 'Then when I was eighteen Mama mentioned that we needed to know the location of Gabriella's father on a particular night, and could I perhaps find out? I knew, deep down. After that night in Naples, I suspected. There was a reason why she wanted that information and that the reason wasn't going to be good. But I was so completely her creature that I ignored my doubts. I took Gabriella out and I got the information I needed from her. I knew she had feelings for me, and I used them the way my mother used mine for her.'

His heart clenched tight at the memory. Of Gabriella's pretty face and the way she'd looked at him, as if the sun rose and set in his eyes. 'It was easy. She told me everything, because she trusted me. And I betrayed her. I passed the information on to my mother.' He'd been so oblivious. So stupid. So blinded. 'Two days later Gabriella's father was killed in a hit carried out by unknown assailants.'

Lucy's eyes widened and he could see the shock in them. Now it was his turn to face judgment, and it would happen. She would soon see his own special brand of hypocrisy.

'Gabriella knew what had happened. She knew that I'd betrayed her. But she didn't blame me. She blamed herself instead.'

Lucy's hand pressed hard against his chest, as if she could sense his self-loathing and wanted to ease the burn of it. But nothing would. Nothing would ever make that get any better. Only the fire of justice ever came close.

'I was complicit in her father's death,' he said flatly, so there could be no mistake. 'I'd ignored the doubts I'd had for years about my mother, too blinded by my love for her to think that everything she'd told me about our family, about myself, could be a lie. But after Gabriella's father died I couldn't ignore it any longer.' He remembered the weight of his own realisation. The crushing burden of understanding that had nearly annihilated him. 'I confronted my mother about it and she laughed. Told me it was just business. That if I wanted to remain part of the family I should get used to it. That I'd already done so much to help, after all…'

He gritted his teeth, remembering his mother's warm, familiar smile. And the cold, cold look in her eyes. 'It was a threat and we both knew it. A reminder that I was as guilty as she and that she had the power to do something about it if I became a problem.' His mouth moved in a smile, though there was no humour at all in it. 'It was common knowledge that there was only one way out of the de Santi family and that was in a box.'

Lucy's gaze was dark and liquid, but she didn't say anything.

'So I made a decision.' He could still feel the flame of that decision, burning hot and strong. It never went out. He couldn't afford to let it. 'I gathered all the pieces of information I could find on my mother's activities and I forwarded them to the police. I made sure I was at her trial to give evidence and I made sure she went to prison. She didn't look at me at all as they led her away. I was dead to her already.'

There were so many things that had scarred him in that moment. The knowledge that he'd negotiated his own immunity from prosecution by betraying his mother. An immunity he'd wanted so he could dedicate his life to pursuing his own justice.

The way she'd ignored him so completely. He didn't blame her in the end, but it had hurt all the same. Confirmation, as if he'd needed it, that he'd never been her son to love.

There was silence afterwards, but he couldn't hear anything above the pounding of his own heartbeat.

'If I can't blame myself for what happened with my mother, then you can't blame yourself for what happened with yours, Vincenzo,' Lucy said quietly. 'You weren't complicit. You were used.'

CHAPTER NINE

VINCENZO'S DARK EYES were full of fire. 'You think I don't know that?'

'I do think you know that.' The anger in his face told her that clearly. 'But you don't feel it, do you?' She'd phrased it as a question, but it wasn't meant to be one. Not when she knew the truth so intimately herself. 'You feel responsible.'

'Of course I feel responsible. I lured that woman to that van. And I used my friendship with Gabriella to betray her father. My actions caused his death, and I knew all along that something wasn't right about it. I knew all along that there was doubt. But I didn't listen to that doubt. I didn't listen to my instinct. And if I had—'

'If you had, what would have changed?' She didn't know why she was arguing with him. It was only that there was pain in his heart the way there was in hers, and that he blamed himself just as she blamed herself. They were so alike. Both children of monsters. It made her feel his agony as if it were her own. 'You might have saved him, but someone else might have got hurt instead. And if the past doesn't matter for me, then it can't matter for you. We can't be complicit when both our parents used us, and we can't change what happened.'

His expression had become hard, like stone, but his eyes glittered, sharp as volcanic glass. 'No, I can't. Which is why the only thing of importance is what I do now. And that is taking down the people like my mother. Those families who have caused so much harm to so many people. Justice is the only way forward.'

And he was burning with it, that was clear.

Foreboding fluttered deep inside her, but she ignored it. She understood all too well where he was coming from and she could see how heavily guilt weighed on him. Gabriella hadn't blamed him, but he blamed himself, and that surely had to be an impossible burden.

You know about those too.

Oh, yes, she did. She'd carried the weight of her mother's death for a long time, after all. But this life he'd set out for himself, this crusade, had to be a lonely one. She knew better than anyone how difficult it must be, to be constantly on your guard, to never feel safe. Never to be able to trust anyone.

Her heart ached for him and there was nothing she could do. No words to make the burden he bore for the deaths of those people lighter, no way to ease it. All she could do was offer him understanding, because she carried those same burdens.

He'd told her that she wasn't to blame and that she was worth saving, but the feeling in her heart was still the same, the doubt and the fear.

He felt those things too.

Maybe, though, there was some help she could offer him...

She shifted in his lap. 'Wait here. I'll be a couple of minutes.' Before he could stop her or ask what she was doing, she'd slipped off him, going quickly into the house and to her bedroom. Her laptop was still sitting in her bag on the armchair near the bed, so she got it out and went back to the terrace.

Vincenzo had risen to his feet, that dark menace gathering around him again, staring at her fiercely. But she ignored him. She opened up the laptop and typed in her password, then opened up the files she'd encrypted only a week ago.

Then she held out the laptop to him. 'Here. All the information you need about my father is in this file. It's yours, Vincenzo.'

He didn't look at it or make any move to take it. 'You were going to give me that at the end of the week. That was the deal.'

'I know. But justice is important to you, and I don't want to cower in fear any more. I want to do something. I want to help.'

'But why now? Why not before?'

'Because I understand better now why you're doing it and where you're coming from. And I don't want to keep that information from you. More people could get hurt the longer I hold on to it, and I don't want that either.' She lifted her chin, held that fierce stare. 'Take what's on that laptop. Use it to put him behind bars for the rest of his life, because that's what he deserves. At the very least for my mother's sake. And at the end of this weekend I won't protest. I'll go quietly to the authorities.'

Still he didn't take the laptop.

'If I have the information now, what's to stop me from handing you over immediately?'

He wouldn't, though. She knew in her bones that he wouldn't.

'You won't.' She dared him to contradict her. 'You gave me your word and I think that's important to you too.'

Once again he said nothing, that look on his face like a judge debating a sentence. 'You're really prepared to give yourself up? Just like that?'

That he didn't deny it caused her heart to miss a beat, just once. But she ignored it, because what else could she do? After all the things he'd told her about himself and his motivations? His reasons for what he was doing? He was taking responsibility for his actions and trying to make amends, and she couldn't fault that. She couldn't pretend that she didn't have amends to make either because, although logically she knew she wasn't responsible for her mother's death, the guilt remained. And maybe answering for the crimes she'd committed afterwards would help ease it.

'You've devoted your life to justice, Vincenzo. You took responsibility for yourself and the wrongs your mother did, and you're making up for that harm by preventing harm to others. By stopping those responsible. Yet what have I done? I broke the law and my actions would have caused people pain.' That guilt was so heavy, weighing her down. 'I need to pay for that. I don't want to go to jail, but not wanting to doesn't put me above the law. And besides… I don't want to manipulate you into helping me escape. That would be forcing you to compromise your principles and I can't ask that of you.'

He had set her an example and all she could do was follow it. She couldn't claim a freedom that she didn't deserve, and she couldn't ask him to ignore everything he believed in just for her sake.

Slowly, Vincenzo reached for the laptop and took it from her. But even then he didn't look at it. He put it down on the stone bench and reached for her, drawing her close. He was so tall she had to tilt her head back to look up at him. Her glasses were still on the arm of the bench, but she didn't need them to see those burning, dark eyes, and the expression on his face, like stone.

What he was thinking, she had no idea.

She didn't know whether she still wanted him to change his mind, or whether she'd be happier in a jail cell. Either way it seemed she'd have to endure pain, so perhaps it was better that she didn't know what he was thinking. Perhaps it was better to just be in the moment with him, where there was only his warmth and strength. The way he looked at her and the way he touched her. Where there was no past and no future.

Only them. Together.

He lifted his hands and cupped her face between them, staring at her as if she was a book in a language he didn't know but had always wanted to learn.

'*Civetta,*' he said softly, 'why should my principles matter to you?'

Honesty was precious, he'd told her, and so honesty she'd give him, even though perhaps telling him this wasn't wise. Even though she was still sorting through the implications of it for herself.

'It's not your principles.' Her voice was scraped and raw. 'It's you, Vincenzo. You matter to me.'

She wasn't sure when it had happened, when

he'd suddenly become important to her, but he had. And perhaps she'd only come to the real-isation in the last ten minutes or maybe she'd known subconsciously for days. Whatever, the when didn't matter. She only knew that she felt it now, like a fire burning hot and strong inside her. A fire that in the space of the last half-hour, as they'd shared their secrets, had only strengthened.

You cannot feel anything for him, remember?

Oh, she remembered. But this was merely a feeling of...kinship. Nothing more than that.

Shock flickered in his gaze and something else, an instinctive heat that made her breath catch. His palms were warm against her skin, resting there lightly, holding her gently. Yet there was nothing gentle or light about the way he looked at her. Angry, almost. As if he hadn't liked her answer one bit.

'Don't.' An underlying thread of ferocity wound through his cool voice. An order that he wanted her to obey. 'You can't let me matter, Lucy. You can't feel anything for me, under-stand? I negotiated immunity from my crimes so I could dedicate myself to bringing people to justice, and that's my sentence. And it's for life. I cannot be distracted from it, not by you. Not by anyone.'

It was a warning, but she didn't need it. She knew what was at stake already. Not that there was any kind of future for them even if she'd wanted there to be. He wouldn't compromise his principles and she would never ask him to.

Yet they could have this moment and perhaps a night. Perhaps even the next couple of days, too. Surely that wouldn't be too much to ask?

Her mother had wanted her to be happy, and she'd never been happier in her life than when was in his arms.

'I know,' she said. 'Believe me, I know. But I think we could have the next couple of days, couldn't we?'

An expression she couldn't name rippled over his face. 'Oh, *civetta,* I don't—'

'Please, Vincenzo.' She stared up into the inky darkness of his eyes. 'I've never been happy before, but you've given me a taste of it. And I wouldn't mind a little more to take with me when I go.'

He muttered something harsh under his breath, the glitter in his eyes full of anger and desire, heat and regret, and too many other things she didn't understand.

But she understood the demand of his kiss as he bent his head and took her mouth, hard and deep and hot. Knew, too, the taste of his desperation, because she felt the same. She put her arms around his neck, rose up on her toes, kissing him back just as desperately as he was kissing her. And everything suddenly became feverish and raw.

He swept her up into his arms, carrying her from the terrace and through the villa till they reached his bedroom, where he tore the robe from her body and laid her on the bed. He got rid of his clothes, found the protection they needed, then eased apart her thighs and settled himself between them.

He didn't wait and she didn't need him to. There was a yawning emptiness inside her, an echoing hollow space that only he could fill. And he did, thrusting deep and hard inside her. And this time he didn't treat her as if she was made of glass. He didn't go softly or gently, treating her as if she was vulnerable.

He gripped her thighs, hauling them up and around his waist, tilting her hips back so he could slide more completely inside her, and then he was moving in an almost savage rhythm, forceful and hard and demanding.

It felt so good. Exactly what she wanted. Because she wasn't the scared little girl he'd brought to Capri days ago. She was different now. She was changed. She wasn't afraid any more, not of herself and not of him, and not of what she wanted.

And she wanted everything. She wanted it all and now, because she didn't have long to enjoy it. Only a few days. But she would take those days and throw herself into them. Take as much happiness as he could give her and then come back for more. She wouldn't hold back and she'd deny him nothing.

She might not deserve it, but he did. Everything he'd given her she'd give back to him, because, whether he knew it or not, he needed it too.

So she put her arms around him and tightened her thighs around his hips, holding him to her, moving with him. And she kissed him, nipped him, licked him. Let him know how much she liked what he was doing to her, how much she wanted all the pleasure he gave her.

And when she'd reached the point of desperation, when her soul had been drawn so tight with pleasure she almost couldn't stand it, she stared up into his intense face, and felt everything inside her still.

It was as if he held her in the palm of his hand, her whole being gathered up tight in his fist. Then he opened his fingers and her soul flew free, caught in a spiralling ecstasy. Only to fall into the hot darkness of his eyes.

And drown there.

For the first time in his life, Vincenzo had no idea what to do. Always, his path had been clear to him. Always, he knew in which direction to turn and which route to take.

Justice was what he was after. Justice for the woman he'd lured into that dark alleyway. Justice for Gabriella and her father. And perhaps some justice for himself, too. For the way he'd been used and manipulated.

There had never been any conflict within him. He always knew that what he was doing was the right thing, and even when there had been protests and denials from the people he'd put away, he'd never doubted that they deserved what they got.

But now he was made of doubt and the path that had always been so clear was shrouded in fog.

Lucy had accepted that she was guilty of the crimes she'd committed for her father and that Vincenzo would turn her over to the police. And not just accepted it. She felt she deserved it.

Days earlier, there had been none of this conflict. Yes, she was guilty. Yes, she deserved it. But now…things were different.

He sat on a sun lounger under the shade of a big white linen umbrella, gazing at the woman who lay face down on the lounger next to him, her head buried in the crook of one arm, her mass of dark hair in drifts over her pale shoulders. Beyond was the cool blue of the pool built right on the edge of the cliff, and beyond that the deeper blue of the sea dotted with white sails.

The past couple of days they'd done nothing but make love, eat, talk, swim, before starting back at the beginning again. He'd wanted to take her for a tour of the island, but the safety concerns were significant and he didn't want her to feel hemmed in by his security staff, so he'd organised to take her out on his small yacht, which at least gave her the illusion of freedom and meant they could be by themselves, even if his staff followed along behind them in another launch at a discreet distance.

She'd loved that, sitting out on the deck in the sun with the wind in her hair. Then he'd got her to take the wheel while he stood behind her, his hands guiding hers as she steered the little yacht. She'd laughed with delight, leaning back against him as they guided the yacht through the waves. The wind had been up and they'd moved fast, which had thrilled her.

Afterwards, after they'd talked more, sharing pieces of their childhoods that weren't too fraught as they'd eaten the lunch Martina had given them, he'd anchored in a sheltered, private bay and they'd gone swimming off the boat. Then, still wet and salty from the water, he'd taken her down onto the deck and made love to her under the sails as the boat rocked gently.

'I've never been happy before,' she'd told

him the night she'd handed him her laptop, '*but you've given me a taste of it...*'

He'd given her a taste of that happiness. He, who'd only ever delivered justice, had made someone happy. And she'd wanted more of it, so she'd have something good to take with her when she went to jail...

The thought of that was unbearably painful for reasons he couldn't describe even to himself. Because why should he care whether she was happy or not? And why did he want to be the one who gave her that happiness?

Why did he even think she deserved it? She'd hidden her father's money and had enabled him to make more, helping him build the crime empire he now commanded whether she'd been aware of it or not. She'd helped him evade the law and she'd known that was wrong.

Yes, she did deserve a prison cell.

But she'd also watched her mother bleed to death. A death she held herself responsible for. And she'd lived in fear for years afterwards, threatened and terrorised, deprived of companionship and love and happiness, everything that made life worth living.

She'd been forced into doing things that went

against her loving, loyal and honest nature, things that might have broken another person. But Lucy hadn't broken. She'd made a promise to the mother who'd died to protect her and had survived any way she could. He couldn't fault her for that. But it had left scars on her. The weight of a guilt she couldn't escape, just as he couldn't.

Lucy sighed and stretched on the sun lounger. She'd been wearing a swimsuit, but after their last swim, when he'd stripped it off her and had her up against the wall of the pool, she hadn't bothered to put it on again, and so was lying there naked, her pale skin flushed in the sunlight.

His beautiful *civetta*...

She doesn't deserve that cell and you know it.

His chest felt tight, as if his heart was pressing hard against his ribcage, a strong, steady ache. He felt as if he was looking through a window that had once been crystal clear, but had fogged up, rendering the view indistinct and out of focus. He couldn't even work out what he was looking at now. A badly hurt innocent or a criminal who deserved prison?

She was both, and that was the issue. That was why he didn't know what to do.

She is you, you realise that, don't you?

Vincenzo abruptly shut the laptop he'd been working on, the constriction in his chest getting tighter. No, surely not. She wasn't him.

She didn't have a history of corruption of her own family and she hadn't actually led people to their deaths as he had.

You think she should pay for her crimes while you escape having to pay for yours?

He *was* paying for his crimes. What he'd told her that night was the truth. He was serving a life sentence, using his contacts and his knowledge to help the police. Dedicating his life to the pursuit of justice.

He'd put a lot of people behind bars, more than if he'd been rotting in a cell himself. And it wasn't as if the life he had now had anything to do with freedom. Yes, he had money and a life of ease, but he lived in a cage all the same. A gilded one. Hemmed in by security, since not a day went by when someone didn't make an attempt on his life. Isolated, since he could trust nothing and no one. Curtailed in everything he did because, as far as he was concerned, everything had one point and one point only: justice.

He had paid and he was still paying. He'd be paying for the rest of his life.

Fine, but do you really think she should? Hasn't she paid already?

Putting the laptop down on the table beside him, he got off the lounger and paced over the green lawn towards the stone parapet that stood between him and the cliff face.

Her life had been a misery, spent in fear and loneliness, and so really she *had* paid. She'd been forced into committing offences and, regardless of what he'd told himself about choices, Lucy hadn't had one. Was she really guilty? And did she really deserve to be handed over to the authorities?

But then, what would he do with her if he didn't? She'd asked him to help her escape, find a new life for herself in the States…

Or you could keep her.

A fist closed around his heart, squeezing him tight, making it so he could hardly breathe.

He could keep her. She could live here in the villa. With him.

Slowly, Vincenzo turned around, his gaze settling on her where she lay on the sun lounger, a primitive sense of possession filling him. Perhaps he wouldn't give her up. Perhaps he would keep her. She would be there whenever he wanted her, warm and silky and sweet. Giving him her honesty and her passion. Her loyalty and her trust. He wouldn't have to be alone any more. He would have her.

And why not? He was paying for his crimes, but why couldn't he have something for himself? And it wouldn't be only for himself. It would be for her too, because she'd told him that he was important to her, and surely staying with him was more important to her than being imprisoned in a cell?

Is that really what she needs, though? And isn't being trapped on this island with you really just another cell?

A chill washed over him, burning away the burst of possessiveness. It was true, he could keep her here with him. And he could make her happy, he was sure. In fact, perhaps he even should, since with her help he'd be able to take down even more people than he would on his own.

But what kind of life would that be for her?

She'd be in constant danger from those looking to use her to get to him, unable to go anywhere without security. It would be a curtailed, narrow sort of life.

It was the life she'd escaped when she'd run from her father. The life her mother had told her to get free of.

You can't do that to her.

Over on the sun lounger, Lucy sighed and turned her head, her hair trailing down her back. He could see her face, naked without her glasses, and for the first time he didn't see vulnerability and fear there. Her eyes were closed and her mouth was curved slightly in a satisfied way, and she looked at peace. She looked… happy.

He could give her more of that here, but not for ever. She was curious and intelligent and he could imagine her living a life without fear, where she was free to explore everything that interested her. Where she could put those impressive financial skills to better use in a way that would fulfil her, not cause her guilt and pain.

But that life wasn't with him. He'd chosen his path and it was a solitary one; he couldn't make her walk it with him. And if he couldn't trap her in a cage here with him, he couldn't trap her in any other cage either.

The knowledge filtered through him, not fast like a lightning strike but slowly, like the sun rising.

He couldn't give her to the authorities. He couldn't let her go to prison.

Yes, she'd broken the law but there were extenuating circumstances. She'd lost so much and there was so much good she could do out in the world. So much good she *would* do, because of the kind of person she was.

What things could she do if she was allowed to follow her own passions? What kinds of things could she create if she weren't hemmed in by fear?

What kind of person could she become?

Ah, but he knew already. She would be amazing.

He couldn't keep that from her. He wouldn't.

It went against everything he'd thought justice was, but maybe there were more forms of justice in this world than he'd previously thought. And besides, it would be a greater injustice to put her back in a cage than it would be to take her out of it.

Determination sat inside him, a new sense of purpose.

He'd never wanted anything more from this life than to bring down the people who hurt others and he would keep on with doing that. She'd brought him a little space of peace and he would remember that for ever.

But she wasn't his and she never would be. And the greatest gift he could give to the world would be to let her go.

Lucy sighed again and rolled over, glancing to where he'd been sitting. She frowned when she didn't see him, sitting up and looking around.

Then her gaze found his and her face lit up, and she smiled.

No, *that* was the sun rising. That was the lightning strike. Her and her smile, and the way she looked at him. As if he was a sight that made her happy and gave her joy.

Then she held out her arms to him and he felt something inside him crumble and fall away, like a narrow cliff path collapsing under his feet. There was nothing to stop him, nothing to hold on to. One moment the path was firm and solid, the next he was in the air and he was falling.

It was dizzying, terrifying, a rush of intense happiness and hope, along with a despair that he hadn't felt since he'd betrayed Gabriella.

He didn't know how he was ever going to give his *civetta* up.

But he was going to have to.

CHAPTER TEN

LUCY PAUSED BESIDE the bed and briefly debated whether to grab the book she'd been reading to bring down to the pool, or the financial magazine Vincenzo had given her. The book was some nice escapism, but the magazine had some interesting articles, and she wasn't sure what she was in the mood for. Both, perhaps?

She picked them up and turned to the door just as Vincenzo strode in.

A delicious shiver worked its way down her spine the way it always did whenever he was near, her heart beating faster, tension and flutters of heat collecting in the pit of her stomach. Along with a desperate, tight feeling she couldn't shake.

He was in a perfectly tailored midnight-blue suit today, with a black shirt that only emphasised his compelling, dark magnetism. With his inky hair and obsidian eyes, the harsh planes and angles of his face, he was the most beautiful man she'd ever seen in her life.

Don't feel anything for him. You can't.

No, of course she didn't. She was just…admiring him. And she liked being near him and touching him and having him look at her. She was happy whenever she was in his presence, so happy…

But it was nothing more than that. And it certainly wasn't love.

She smiled and took a step towards him, but he didn't smile back. And he didn't reach for her the way he normally did. The expression on his face was carved from stone, his black eyes cold. He looked the way he had when she'd first seen him in his office nearly a week ago. Unyielding. Ruthless…

A chill crept through her.

'Is there something wrong?' She tried a smile, hoping he would smile back, let her know that everything was fine. 'I was just going down to the pool and—'

'It's time to pack, Lucy.' His voice was cool. 'You'll be leaving in an hour.'

She was aware of a rushing sound in her ears, her vision tunnelling, darkness creeping in around the edges. 'What do you mean, leaving? You gave me your word that—' She stopped dead as he thrust out his hand.

He held something small, square and blue.

A passport. A United States passport.

The rushing in her ears grew louder, her vision wavering, her breath coming short and hard. She didn't understand. Why was he giving her a passport?

You know why.

She had an inkling. It was what she'd asked for when she'd initially come to him: an escape. To disappear to a new life in the States. With a new name and identity so no one would ever find her. Where she would be safe at last, just as her mother had wanted.

But that was before she'd realised he would never let her go the way she'd hoped. Before she'd accepted the weight of her own guilt and her need to make amends for the crimes she'd committed for her father. She'd accepted that her future was a cell and, if she wasn't exactly happy about it, she wouldn't balk at it either.

Except this was…not a cell. This was the escape she'd come to him to help her find.

'I don't understand.' Her voice sounded

hoarse. She glanced at the passport in his hand and then at him. 'What does this mean?'

'What do you think it means?' There was only granite in the words, the hard edge of stone. 'I'm not handing you over to the authorities, Lucy. I've organised a passport for you with a new identity, visas, social security numbers, everything you'll need to start a new life in the States. Your father will never find you, I'll make sure of it.'

She began to shake, the tremors starting in her stomach and moving outwards, to her hands and knees. This surely couldn't be happening. He couldn't be giving her freedom. Not after everything he'd told her about justice and making amends. About guilt and the law and taking responsibility.

'But…' She tried to make sense of what was happening. 'I was going to be handed over to the authorities. That's what you were going to do and I—'

'I changed my mind.' His voice was like a blade, cutting her off. 'I'm not going to hand you over to the police.'

'Why not?' She searched his face to find some signs of his reasoning, but there was nothing. His features were stone. 'You were very clear that's what you were going to do. I don't understand why you're changing your mind.'

'You were forced into doing those things for your father, Lucy. You had no choice. And even if you had, you've paid many times over for those crimes.'

'But I haven't,' she said hoarsely.

'Haven't you?' His gaze cut like a knife. 'Weren't the years you spent as your father's prisoner a jail term? Wasn't that house he kept you in a cell? He took your mother from you, *civetta*. And that is a life sentence.'

She felt as if the ground had shifted under her feet. As if she were walking in quicksand that would suck her down at any moment. She'd never thought he'd change his mind. Never thought he'd present her with the freedom she wanted, enabling her to keep the promise she'd made to her mother long ago. A freedom she didn't deserve…

Is that really true, though?

Something hot swept through her. He'd told her she wasn't responsible, that she couldn't blame herself, that she was worth saving, and then, over the course of the past couple of days, he'd shown her. He'd taken care of her, made her feel valued, made her feel precious, and more—he made her feel worth the sacrifice her mother had made for her.

'You are worth saving, Lucy Armstrong...' he'd told her, and he'd believed it. This beautiful, passionate, strong man who'd changed her, healed her...

She stared at him and the ground kept shifting, the landscape kept changing, that hot, bright emotion continuing to sweep through her, crushing everything in its path. It was raw and intense and it filled her with strength, made her feel ten feet tall and bulletproof.

And she knew what it was. She knew the truth deep in her heart, in her soul.

The feeling was love.

Was this what her mother had felt when she'd protected her? This sweep of power? Blinding and sure and so utterly certain. A burst of purity, filling her with a confidence she'd never dreamed she'd have.

She'd been so afraid of this feeling all this time. Afraid of its power. The kind of power that made someone stay with someone who hurt them. That made them give up their lives for someone else. But she understood now, she got it.

Love wasn't something to fear, it was something to embrace. Because love was strength and it was courage, and that was what her mother had drawn on to take that blow to protect her. Her love for her daughter.

Lucy's eyes filled with sudden tears. She couldn't let that sacrifice be in vain. Her mother hadn't just wanted a life for her, she'd wanted her to be happy. And that was the best monument, wasn't it? Happiness? Not just for her, but for him too, because they'd both been through terrible things and they deserved it.

They deserved to have a future. And it would be love that would give them that future.

She met Vincenzo's hard, midnight gaze. 'No,' she said.

He ignored her. 'Pack your things. You'll be leaving in an hour.'

'No,' she repeated.

Vincenzo's expression became even harder than it already was. 'No? What do you mean, no?'

Lucy looked him in the eye. 'I mean no. I'm not leaving. I want to stay.'

The expression on his face darkened. 'This was what you wanted, Lucy. A new life. That's what you promised your mother.'

'Well, that's not what I want now.' And she didn't hesitate. She gave him the truth, because that was always what she gave him. 'What I want is you.'

A muscle flicked in his jaw, tension gathering around him like a storm gathering electricity. *'Civetta...'*

'I want the moments I'd planned. I want another day. I want more than that. I want a future, Vincenzo. I want a future with you.'

The tension around him became even more electric, a subtle vibration in the air. 'No.' The word left no room for argument. 'You will go and you will go now.'

'Why not?' She took a step towards him, holding his black gaze. 'Don't you want a future too?'

'No.' Something broke in him, the stillness shattering.

He threw the passport onto the bed suddenly, then he closed the distance between them in an explosive movement, reaching for her, his fingers closing around her upper arms and holding her in a grip that bordered on painful. It might have frightened her once, but there was nothing about him that frightened her now, and certainly not with the emotion blazing in his dark eyes, a black fire that nearly swallowed her whole.

'Yes,' he said roughly. 'Yes, I want that. I want a future. I want for ever with you, *civetta*. But if I take even one day I will *never* let you go. Do you understand now?'

Her heart was full, emotion flooding out of her, and she didn't hide it. She let him see what was in her soul.

'Then don't.' She leaned into his strong grip and his heat. Leaning into him. 'Don't let me go.'

For a second the fire in his eyes blazed so hot it nearly burned her to the ground, the grip he had on her searing her. But that was okay. She wanted to burn. She wanted to burn with him.

But then, as abruptly as he'd grabbed her, he let her go and stepped away, leaving her swaying, leaning into a warmth that was no longer there. The fire in his eyes had gone, the blaze doused. He was cold again, expressionless. Emotionless.

'You say that,' he said, casual. 'But you don't understand what your life would be like with me. People want to kill me every day. I'm a target and so you'll be a target too. You won't be able to go anywhere without a security detail or without planning your every movement. Your life will be curtailed. The only place you'll ever have any freedom is here in the villa, with me.'

'So?' She smiled, wanting him to understand. 'None of that matters, Vincenzo. Don't you see?'

His eyes were black stars, glittering cold and sharp. 'No, I don't see. And you may not think it matters, but it matters to me. I don't want you to be a prisoner with me on this island. I don't want you to have a life limited by safety concerns and security. You should be free to explore the things that interest you, that excite you. And, more than anything, you should be safe. And I can't give you that. I can never give you that.'

A crack ran slowly through her heart, sharp and jagged. Because it was obvious that he didn't understand. And why would he? He'd been betrayed by someone who loved him, the person who'd mattered most. No one had protected him the way her mother had protected her. She might have lost her mum, but she'd known that Kathy had loved her. Had he had anyone who'd cared about him?

He was so hard, so cold. So shut down. All the passion she knew lived in him locked away... No, he hadn't.

'Vincenzo—'

'I don't want to hear it. That is my decision, whether you like it or not.'

She studied him, sensing the battle in him. He'd been at war with himself the whole time she'd been here, torn between his principles and his passions. But he didn't have to choose, couldn't he see that? Didn't he know? He could have both. Love was big enough.

He's afraid.

The insight came almost forcibly and she saw it, because she knew fear, knew it intimately. It was there in his eyes, in the lies he was telling himself and her. And they were lies. He was afraid of what was between them and he didn't know what to do.

'If you really wanted me, you could have me,' she said quietly. 'It doesn't have to be a choice, Vincenzo. It's not one or the other. It's not black and white. And all this stuff about keeping me safe sounds good, but it's just a convenient excuse, isn't it?'

He said nothing, the tension around him almost humming.

The crack in her heart became deeper, wider, and her eyes prickled with tears. Because he was desperate, she could feel it. He was fighting so hard, her poor Vincenzo, and she didn't know what to say to reach him. To show him that he had nothing to fear.

She took a step closer, but he didn't move, towering over her, his gaze utterly forbidding. Intimidating. Yet she knew better now what that aura of menace actually was. It was his armour, his protection. His heart had been broken into pieces once before and now he was desperately shielding it.

'It's okay,' she said softly, trying to calm him the way he'd calmed her days ago. 'It's all right. You don't have to be afraid.'

His eyes glittered, cold as the depths of space. 'I'm not afraid. You deserve freedom, Lucy. And what I deserve is freedom from you. You're a distraction. You're getting in the way and taking up my time. I have more important things to do than sleep with you.'

It might have hurt her badly if she'd been the same Lucy that had come to Capri days before. But she wasn't the same Lucy. She was changed, and he'd changed her. He'd shown her where her true strength lay, and it wasn't running and hiding, it was in embracing what was in her heart. And she knew he was lying. That what he was doing was protecting himself. He was a city under siege and he would do anything he could to keep the invaders out.

And she could storm those walls with anger and pain, but she knew that wouldn't work. It would only make him call for reinforcements. No, if she wanted to crack his defences she was going to have to drop her own.

Lucy reached out and gently touched his cheek, the faintest brush of her fingers. 'I've fallen in love with you, did you know that?' The words were soft, yet the power of the feeling inside her vibrated in every syllable. 'You make me so happy.'

And just for a second the walls around his city looked as if they might shatter as shock flickered through his black eyes. The defenders putting down their swords, the battle inside him pausing.

But only for a moment.

'I don't care,' he said in a voice made of ice.

The crack through her heart became a chasm. He couldn't see, he couldn't understand. Because he didn't want to.

Vincenzo de Santi was a man with an iron will and he'd made a decision and nothing was going to sway him, still less the woman who loved him with everything she was.

He was happy in his cage. He didn't want to see that she was handing him a key.

Anger and pain would accomplish nothing. Only love could scale those walls. Only love would help him overcome his fear. But it was something he would have to come to in his own time. He would have to open the gates of his heart himself—she couldn't force him.

It hurt. It hurt so much. But her pain wasn't for herself, it was for him. This beautiful, powerful, passionate panther, stuck in a cage of his own making. Too afraid of the open door standing before him to take a step through it.

All she could do was give him what she always gave him: the truth. And hope that somehow it would stay with him. It would be her last gift to him.

'If that's what you choose to believe, then fine,' she said quietly. 'But know this. All the justice in the world won't change the feeling inside you. It won't do anything for the guilt or the grief. But you can allow yourself to have something good. You can let yourself be happy. You deserve it, Vincenzo. And so do I.'

He said nothing, cold radiating from him so fiercely he might as well have been made of ice, but she went on anyway.

'I think you do care. I think you love me as much as I love you. But you're afraid and I think I understand why. You were betrayed by the one person who shouldn't have betrayed you and now you're protecting yourself.' She wanted to touch him again, but she couldn't bring herself to do it, not when she knew it wouldn't help. 'But I need you to know right now that you can trust me. I won't betray you. I love you and you don't have to be worthy of that love. You don't have to be pure. You don't have to be just. You don't have to prove yourself, not to me. The only thing you have to be is you.'

The silence that fell was deafening.

Vincenzo's gaze had turned flat and black and depthless. 'Are you done?'

'Yes,' she said and her voice didn't shake, even though her heart had cracked into pieces in her chest.

This time he said nothing.

He simply turned on his heel and left.

He didn't want to see her pack up her meagre belongings. Didn't want to see her tears or hear her husky, sweet voice telling him things he didn't want to hear. Telling him that he was afraid. That she loved him.

So he left her standing there, going down to his office and slamming the door.

Rage burned in his heart. At himself for what he couldn't let himself have and at her for all those things she'd said. Because he wasn't afraid. And he really didn't care. And as for worthiness...

Vincenzo strode to his desk and sat down, preparing to focus on some work, trying to shove all those thoughts from his head.

But it was impossible.

'You don't have to be worthy,' she'd said, as

if he'd been trying to make himself worthy all this time. Which wasn't true. He *knew* he wasn't worthy. What he was doing was trying to atone. For himself and for his family. Pursuing justice was the only way he could make up for what he'd done, for the weight of guilt that crushed him.

'All the justice in the world won't change the feeling inside you...'

Ah, but she was wrong about that too. He'd wait until she'd vanished to the States and was safely ensconced in the new life he'd made for her, letting her father believe she was still with him on Capri. And only once she was settled would he make his move.

And that *would* make him feel better. Delivering justice to the man who'd hurt her.

You, you mean?

Vincenzo gritted his teeth. Yes, sending her away had hurt her, but he'd had to do it. And it wasn't because of fear. He'd told her the truth; he couldn't allow her to distract him from his true purpose, because what else would he be without it?

A liar. A murderer. A traitor. A tool to be used, not a son to be loved.

'You were betrayed by the one person who was supposed to love you...'

His *civetta*. She knew exactly what to say to appeal to his traitorous emotions. And they were traitorous. He couldn't trust them.

But she loves you. She won't betray you.

A spear of ice caught him in the chest, the pain so sharp he could hardly breathe, along with a raw, desperate feeling that made him want to run from his office and find her. Hold on to her. Cup her white face between his palms and kiss away the tears on her cheeks and the pain in her eyes. Give her those moments she wanted, give her the happiness she deserved.

But he'd told her he didn't care that she loved him, and he'd told himself. And he believed it. He *had* to believe it.

So he stayed where he was, his hands clenched in fists on his desk.

In the gardens outside, he could hear the sound of the helicopter's rotors. His security staff would be leading her to the helicopter that would take her to Naples. From there, she'd take the jet to New York. Everything had been organised for her. He wasn't going to leave her in the middle of a foreign city with nothing.

There was a heavy, aching sensation in the centre of his chest. It hurt. He'd never been shot in all the years he'd spent destroying organised crime, but perhaps it felt something a little like this, a bright, pure agony reaching every part of him.

He ignored it. Because she was wrong. Justice *would* cure this pain. He just had to be more focused, concentrate solely on his mission. He had to work harder.

There could not be any more distractions.

He could hear the rotors spinning faster now, faster and faster, and his whole body tightened with the urge to go to the windows and watch the helicopter take off, watch her fly away from him. But he didn't move. Because he didn't care. He wanted her, yes. Needed her, maybe. Love her? No.

She'd told him she loved him as if love was a truth, but she was wrong.

Love was the greatest lie of all.

Love had controlled and manipulated him. Love had blinded him. Duped him. Love had betrayed him.

He would never allow love to have that kind of dominion over him again.

The noise of the helicopter became deafening now as he heard it lift off from the garden, heading into the sky.

Vincenzo closed his eyes as the sound became more and more distant, listening until, at last, it faded away. And there was nothing but silence in his house.

Silence in his heart.

She was gone.

CHAPTER ELEVEN

HE ENDED UP waiting a month. Just until the people he had keeping an eye on Lucy told him she was settled. Her father, naturally, thought she was still with him and had contacted him a number of times, offering all kinds of things for her return.

Vincenzo had ignored all of them.

Once he had confirmation she was safe, he contacted Scotland Yard and gave them everything they needed to bring in Armstrong. And put him away for life.

The news of Armstrong's arrest came swiftly after that, and afterwards Vincenzo sat on the terrace, staring out over the sea, a glass of wine in his hand and the peace of the evening closing in.

It should have been satisfying, but it wasn't.

All he could think about was how empty his villa was. How quiet.

How he wanted to look across this table and

meet a direct hazel gaze, large and dark behind the lenses of her glasses. How he wanted a pair of warm arms to welcome him, and a curvy, silky little body to press itself against him.

How he wanted her smile. Her honesty. Her understanding. Her bluntness and her direct manner.

He wanted her and she wasn't here.

'All the justice in the world won't change the feeling inside you...'

His fingers tightened on his wine glass, the memory of her voice playing in his head.

Over the past month he'd thrown himself into his work, spending hours holed up in his office, sifting through information, looking for his next target.

It should have made him feel better. It should have cleaned the memory of her right out of his head. But it didn't matter how hard he worked, the ache inside him wouldn't go away.

If only that ache was guilt, because that was easier to deal with. But it wasn't. It was her and her absence, the silence around him not one of peace, but of loss.

You made her happy and you sent her away.

Pain deepened in his chest. Happiness. What

was that anyway? He didn't need it himself. He didn't want it. He had a vocation, a calling, and that fulfilled him. It brought him all the satisfaction he required.

'You can let yourself be happy...'

No, he couldn't. Happiness and peace weren't for men like him and she was a fool if she thought they were.

He raised his glass and took a sip, wanting to savour it, but it tasted of nothing. Even the food he ate these days had lost its flavour, just as the world had lost its colour. The sun its warmth...

She'd taken even those small pleasures left to him.

Anger began to burn in his gut, unexpected and fierce, an anger that he'd thought he'd put behind him. And the more he tried to force it away, the more it grew.

She'd done this to him. She'd taken all the little things that had made his life bearable. She'd shown him what peace felt like, what it was to be free of guilt, what it meant to be able to smile at something amusing. She'd shown him how to take a moment and enjoy every second of it.

You made her happy, but she also showed you happiness and now you can never forget it.

The anger burned hotter, flaming high and wild, incinerating everything in its path.

She'd been right, hadn't she? She'd been right all along. Justice would never be enough for him, not now she'd shown him what else he could have, and because he could never have it she'd doomed him.

Vincenzo shoved his chair back so hard it fell over. He rose to his feet, the rage inside him a column of fire, burning him alive. The wine glass was still in his hand, and before he'd even realised what he was doing he'd flung it to the stone floor, crystal exploding in glittering shards.

It was her fault. She'd made him feel like this. And now he'd be Tantalus for ever, desperately thirsty and unable to drink. Starving and unable to eat.

Or you could just accept that what she said was true, that you can let yourself be happy.

Rage coursed through him. How could he accept that? How could he be happy? When he'd hurt people? When he was as guilty as his mother? She was in jail at least, but he wasn't.

You thought Lucy had served her sentence and deserved freedom. Haven't you served yours?

He was shaking, staring unseeing at the remains of the wine glass, glittering in the last rays of twilight. Years he'd spent pursuing his crusade. Years. And still he felt the crushing burden of guilt. That hadn't eased one bit, no matter how many people he had put away. She hadn't lied about that, had she?

No, there had only been one thing that eased him and that was her. Being deep inside her, looking into her eyes. Feeling her arms around him, holding him. Making him feel as if he was more than his mother's broken tool. More than a ruthless, merciless crusader, fighting to fill the gaping void inside him.

The void his mother had left when she walked away from him without a backward glance. The void left by betrayal. Left by love.

He sucked in a breath and then another as the knowledge filtered slowly through him, another truth that Lucy had given him that he'd thought was a lie.

'You're afraid...'

Was he? He hadn't thought he was, but...

What if that was true? What if he just hadn't wanted to believe it? And if that *was* true, then just what the hell was he afraid of?

You know...

Vincenzo closed his eyes. If he didn't have justice, if he didn't have guilt, if he didn't have atonement, then what did he have? Who was he?

Just his mother's tool, her weapon. The puppet she pulled the strings with. An empty void. Unworthy of even her tainted, conditional love.

Fear curled through him, so sharp and bright he shuddered. He didn't want to face it. He wanted to turn and go to his office, lose himself in doing something, anything so this fear didn't choke him. The fear that he was nothing and no one. That he was unworthy, undeserving.

She loves you. She believes you deserve happiness.

What if...she was right? What if his *civetta* had told him the truth? Ah, but then, of course it was the truth. She'd always given him that. So maybe the question wasn't what if she was right? Maybe the question was more what if he believed her?

Something shifted inside him, the urge to run back to his office and bury himself in his crusade. But he knew, with a sudden flash of insight, that if he did that, he'd be doing exactly what he'd been doing for years. Escaping.

Escaping pain. Escaping betrayal. Protecting himself...

Ah, *Dio*, that was what he'd been doing all this time, wasn't it? Running from his fear, running like a coward for decades. Using his justice as his shield and righteousness as his sword.

But he wasn't just or righteous. He was a man cowering in fear. Afraid of his own emotions. Afraid of pain and betrayal. Afraid of the most powerful emotion of all: love.

'I think you love me as much as I love you.'

Vincenzo took a ragged breath, his heart raw, chewed up and spat out, scarred and full of holes, beating hard in his chest as the greatest truth of all settled down inside him. His skin was sensitised, as if the slightest breath of air would cut him to shreds.

Yes, he loved her. He'd loved her for days, for weeks. The entirety of his life had been spent waiting for her and the rest of it would be spent aching for her. She was his fate and his destiny. She was his truth.

And he'd been afraid of her. Afraid of her honesty. Afraid of her strength. Afraid of her courage, because she had more courage and strength in her little finger than he had in his entire body.

And when he'd sent her away he'd been afraid of her love. Afraid of the power of it, of the acceptance and understanding in it. The absolution he could sense it would give him and the happiness and peace it promised him.

He didn't deserve any of those things, but she thought he did. She thought he deserved happiness. She thought he deserved peace. And really, in the end it was a simple choice. He either trusted in her belief, or he didn't.

Ah, but was that even a decision to make? He knew the answer. It lay in his heart, in his soul.

Of course he trusted her. He loved her.

This time, Vincenzo didn't run. He faced his fear. And he accepted her love. Felt it flow through him like a purpose, like a vocation, a calling. Yet so much stronger, so much deeper. So much more complex.

And it wasn't a flame, burning through dry paper, only to crumble to ash when there was nothing to feed it. It was a glow, steady and bright and unending, self-sustaining. True strength in its purest form.

It would never flicker and it would never die. It would be with him always.

Peace came over him, easing the anger, dissipating the last remains of the blaze, cool and soft like Lucy's touch on his skin, a balm to his wounded soul. Bringing with it an absolute certainty.

He would find her. He would lay his heart at her feet. He would give her everything she ever wanted and if what she wanted was to never see him again, he would leave and count it a privilege to have even known her.

It would hurt and he might not survive it, but then, he wouldn't survive without her anyway.

She was more important than justice and she was certainly more important than fear. She was the most important thing in his life and he couldn't let another day pass with her thinking that she wasn't.

Vincenzo reached into his pocket and grabbed

his phone, punching in a number, his hands now steady, the path before him clear and true.

'Get the helicopter now. I'm going to New York.'

Lucy had eventually found herself a little house by the sea in Cape Cod. It wasn't Capri, of course, or the Mediterranean, but the wild Atlantic wasn't far from her door, and there was a beach. And she could walk along that beach, have sand under her toes.

It was a lovely place and she had a job with a small finance firm that enabled her to work from home. It wasn't the most challenging of positions, but she was able to earn a living, which was all she required. She was starting to think longer term, now she had a future ahead of her, and had been toying with the idea of a financial crime consultancy business, but that was still to be decided.

She might even have been happy if it wasn't for the fact that she was missing one thing.

Vincenzo.

She had everything she'd promised her mother she would have. A life away from her father, a life of safety, of freedom.

But she didn't have him. And because she didn't have him, she could never be truly happy. Her heart remained broken and always would.

It was late in the day, the sun going down, and Lucy walked along the beach as she did most late afternoons, her feet sinking into the sand.

She shouldn't give in to these long, solitary walks, because they gave her too much time to think. Too much time to remember how she'd let him turn his back and walk away a month earlier. How she'd collected her things and followed his security staff out to the helicopter, not even watching as it lifted off and flew away because she'd been blinded by tears.

She couldn't force him to see what he didn't want to, and, though love had given her strength, it didn't shield her from the pain of her heart breaking.

Pain for him and what he couldn't allow himself to have.

She remembered the flight to the States and the tears she'd cried for him, weeping herself into sleep at last. Then arriving in New York with an aching throat and gritty eyes.

A kind woman had met her after she'd got off the jet, giving her all the information she needed and showing her to some accommodation in the Village where she could spend a couple of days acclimatising.

She didn't remember that either.

All she remembered was the hollow feeling inside her. Which made sense in a lot of ways, since she'd left her heart in Capri, in Vincenzo de Santi's strong and capable hands.

You just let him have it. You gave it to him and then you walked away.

Lucy bent and picked up a shell, brushing the sand off it.

Of course she had. He'd wanted her to leave and even telling him that she loved him hadn't changed his mind. And not because he didn't want her, but for all those lies he was telling himself. About keeping her safe. About being distracted. About justice.

It was fear and she knew all about fear, how it could get inside you, trap you. And she'd confronted him with his own. But he'd refused to see it. And if he refused to see it, what more could she do? There was nothing.

She stared at the shell, her chest aching. Her

throat tight with grief for the lonely path he'd chosen and the life he'd trapped himself in. He was a prisoner just as much as she'd once been, but his cell was one of his own choosing.

It made her ache.

She lifted her wet face to the sky, letting the tears dry on her cheeks in the wind. And then her gaze narrowed as she saw the tall figure of a man coming down the beach towards her.

It looked like… But no. It couldn't be him. It couldn't be Vincenzo.

She should walk on. The sun would be going down soon and she needed to get home. Yet she didn't move, watching the man walk towards her instead.

Her heart began to speed up, beating wildly in her chest, because it knew who he was, even as her mind balked. And her body tightened, because it knew too. The easy, powerful way he walked. The darkness of his hair. The hard, carved angles of his face…

Lucy stilled. Afraid to move in case he disappeared. Because surely he couldn't be real. Surely he couldn't be here on a beach in Cape Cod. With her.

But he came closer and closer and soon it was

apparent that it was him, and he *was* here, and her heart raged behind her breastbone and she couldn't breathe.

All she could do was stand there as he came to her and, without saying a single word, swept her into his arms.

She stiffened, pushing hard against his solid chest. This couldn't be real. She was dreaming. She'd offered him her heart and he'd refused it.

'Vincenzo? What are you doing here?' And then anger in a cleansing fire hit her and she struggled. 'Let me go.'

He shuddered, as if in pain, and then abruptly his arms opened and she was free. His face was taut with some vast, passionate emotion burning just beneath the surface of his skin, his black eyes blazing with it.

'I need to say something, Lucy,' he said, his voice raw and rough. 'Will you let me?'

She was trembling now, half of her desperate to throw herself back into his arms while the other half was desperate to send him away.

'Say what?' she demanded, shaken and unable to hide it. 'Didn't you say everything you needed to back on Capri?'

'No.' The word was hoarse. 'I didn't. What I said to you then were lies.'

Shock washed through her, the trembling getting worse. 'What lies?'

Vincenzo's gaze was full of something hot and vital, burning steady as the fire at the centre of the earth. 'That you were a distraction. That I didn't care. That I wanted you to leave... You were right, *civetta*. Right about so many things. And it took me a while to see them, to accept what you were trying to tell me, but I know now.' His hands were in fists at his sides, his whole body radiating a familiar tension. 'You told me I was afraid, and you were right. I was. And if you want to know why, it's because of this.' He paused, his great, powerful chest heaving as he sucked in a breath. 'My mother betrayed me. She manipulated me. She took my trust in her, my love for her, and she broke it. She broke me. I was the tool she used to make herself powerful. Not her heir and not her son. Nothing. No one.'

Her heart quivered at the desolation in those words, her eyes filling with tears. 'Oh, Vincenzo. That's not true.'

'I was afraid it was, though, so afraid. I filled

my life up with justice, with a crusade, and used it as an escape, a way to hide. So I didn't have to face the truth that she didn't love me. She never loved me. And perhaps there was nothing in me to love.'

A tear rolled down her cheek, the cracks in her heart aching. 'That's not true,' she said hoarsely. 'There so much in you to love.'

'I didn't believe you back on Capri. I used so many excuses to run from what you were trying to show me. But… I'm tired of running. I'm tired of not believing, of not trusting. I'm tired of filling my life up with something that changes nothing. I want something else, I want something better.' He paused, his eyes dark and full of heat. 'I want you, Lucy Armstrong. You were brave. You facing your fears helped me face mine. And if there's one person in this world I know I can trust, it's you.'

Her throat closed up at the certainty in his face and voice; she couldn't speak.

'You and your honesty and your strength, my *civetta*. You helped me find peace, you gave me a taste of happiness, and I… I want that more than I have wanted anything in my entire life.' The desperate, burning look in his eyes had dissipated, and there was something else there: a steady, bright glow. Calm and sure and certain. 'I'm afraid of being nothing more than what my mother made me, of being no one, and I thought justice would somehow make that feeling go away. But it didn't. It was you who made it go away, Lucy. It was you all this time.' The glow in his eyes became brighter, hotter. 'I love you, my *civetta*. I love you so much. And I know it took me a long time to understand and you will never know how sorry I am that I hurt you, but I can't bear another day of you not being in my life.' Slowly, he raised his arms and held them out, his soul laid bare in his eyes. 'Will you come to me, Lucy? I would very much like you to be mine. And I very much want to be yours.'

There was no thought, only certainty. Only the truth of the feeling that had burned in her heart so long it was part of her.

Lucy closed the distance without hesitation, giving him her answer.

And when his mouth found hers, she knew she'd found everything she'd ever wanted, right there in his arms.

The perfect moment to find her for ever.

The for ever they both deserved and the happiness they'd finally found.

Together.

EPILOGUE

THEY HAD SO many plans. Lucy had informed him of her idea to use her financial skills to help institutions combat fraud and other financial crimes, and so he'd helped her set up a consultancy. As for himself, he'd decided to step away from his crusade. He was going to devote more of himself to his family's auction house and the other various businesses he had. It should keep him busy until they started a family, which they would. After all, someone had to be around to look after the children, and he fully intended to be that someone.

And if he passed on a few titbits that he'd heard through the grapevine to various law enforcement agencies on occasion, then it was only what a fine, upstanding citizen would do.

But the most important plan of all was the wedding Vincenzo had insisted on the moment they returned to Capri.

And that was where he married her, at their villa, the place where they'd both discovered what happiness was. And they discovered it anew as they said their vows to each other in front of the priest.

Lucy wore the most beautiful wedding gown of ivory silk that hugged her curvaceous form, a veil tumbling over her glossy dark curls. They'd been left loose down her spine, but some combs held it back from her lovely face.

No, she was more than lovely. She was beautiful.

She'd given up her glasses today for contact lenses, and not for vanity but because her glasses fogged whenever she cried and she was apparently going to cry a lot—or so she told him.

But she wasn't crying now as he held her small hand and pushed his ring onto her finger. Only looking at him with so much love he could hardly meet her gaze.

Yet meet it he did as he made her his and he became hers.

And he wasn't unworthy or undeserving. He wasn't nothing and he wasn't no one.

He was her husband and he had a new purpose: to love her for the rest of his life.

So he did.

* * * * *

LET'S TALK

Romance

For exclusive extracts, competitions and special offers, find us online:

f facebook.com/millsandboon

⊙ @millsandboonuk

🐦 @millsandboon

Or get in touch on 0844 844 1351*

For all the latest titles coming soon, visit millsandboon.co.uk/nextmonth

*Calls cost 7p per minute plus your phone company's price per minute access charge

Want even more
ROMANCE?

Join our bookclub today!

'Mills & Boon books, the perfect way to escape for an hour or so.'

Miss W. Dyer

'Excellent service, promptly delivered and very good subscription choices.'

Miss A. Pearson

'You get fantastic special offers and the chance to get books before they hit the shops'

Mrs V. Hall

Visit millsandbook.co.uk/Bookclub and save on brand new books.

MILLS & BOON